John Westwood began his career as an actor working in theatre, film, television and voice over. Musical theatre was his first introduction to performing and entertaining. Highlights for John were working with Petula Clark in London's West End and Madonna in a music video. John is a fan of horror movies, especially Hammer horror films with the ultimate Dracula and John's idol Sir Christopher Lee. Years later, he met his idol who became a friend. Another string to his bow! He is an award-winning country singer, and a screenwriter. When he is not writing, he relaxes by painting with acrylics or pastels.

For my very special Mum & Dad
And my sister Tina
With love x

John Westwood

BREEDING

AUSTIN MACAULEY PUBLISHERS™

LONDON · CAMBRIDGE · NEW YORK · SHARJAH

A CIP catalogue record for this title is available from the British Library.

ISBN 9781398480353 (Paperback)
ISBN 9781398480360 (ePub e-book)

www.austinmacauley.com

First Published 2023
Austin Macauley Publishers Ltd®
1 Canada Square
Canary Wharf
London
E14 5AA

Special thanks to my literary agent Steven Lloyd for incredible support.

And Sir Christopher Lee for the inspiration of creating what I am today.

And to my photographer, Diane Sutton.

Table of Contents

Chapter One

St John's Church was built in the 1300s. The stones had worn with age of time and the Cornish coastal air. The tombs and graves were cracked and worn holding stories of their own.

Old yew trees are spread across and around the church holding stories of yesteryear and of ancient worship of druids. Some even say witchcraft and devil worship were used on the grounds and surrounding areas.

Winding narrow roads are well-kept and signs posted all the way to St John's surrounded by overhung trees and bushes that hide the road from any building.

Tonight was a particularly chilly evening and the moon was full in the night sky.

The stars where twinkling against that black canvas and the moon looked larger than normal and so clear you could almost see the craters, well so it seemed.

The church stood bold and silent silhouetted against the light of the moon, the gravcyard was well kept apart from a few headstones that were overgrown and had been neglected over the years of time.

There are three new graves almost next to each other and are clearly visible in the light of the moon. You could just about see the colour of the dirt.

Beneath the dirt lies another story.

Six feet down lays a coffin. Beneath that coffin lid lays the body of a young girl. Skin as pale as ivory and body as cold as ice dressed in a shroud as pale as her skin.

Suddenly her eyes open. She gasps revealing sharp canine fangs.

The wreath on her grave shrivels up and dies in seconds.

***

"You can put that light out now, it's time to go to sleep."

Lewis shuts the book with a thud.

"Oh Mum it was just getting good."

"Lights out, please."

Tanya is a good mum, she lets Lewis get away with almost everything, his father however having that Latin temperament was just a little stricter. Lewis always knew how far to go.

"You heard your mum."

"Yes, Dad."

Lewis puts the book on the floor by the bed and turns out his light.

Carlos is staring out of the French windows of their modest cottage.

"What are you looking at darling?"

"The moon, it's really low tonight."

Tanya joins Carlos and wraps her arms around him looking out at the moon.

"Yes it's really low and so big tonight."

They both stand mesmerised almost hypnotised for just a few moments.

"OK, hot chocolate or Horlicks, what will it be tonight?"

Tanya kisses Carlos on the cheek.

"Oh, I'm in a chocolate mood, dark and hot please."

Carlos laughs then kisses Tanya's nose.

"Just like your man then."

Tanya giggles then sits down on the sofa and grabs a magazine lying on the coffee table.

Flicking through the pages of the TV guide Tanya calls out.

"Do you fancy watching a film?"

Carlos mumbles, "I don't mind."

"What are you eating?"

"A biscuit."

Tanya smiles to herself.

Carlos enters carrying a tray with two mugs and a plate of biscuits.

Carlos has a whole biscuit sticking out of his mouth.

"Oh, you are so romantic."

Carlos sits down next to Tanya on the sofa.

Tanya takes a biscuit and kisses Carlos then pops the biscuit in Carlos's mouth.

Mumbling and juggling the biscuit in his mouth Carlos replies.

"Yep, you know it babe."

Tanya slaps the TV guide.

"Right, what are we going to watch, there is, let me see, Titanic again."

Carlos interrupts. "Oh no that's too long."

Tanya continues looking.

"OK, here we go, what about a good old-fashioned Hammer horror?"

Raising her eyebrows, "The Devil Rides Out?"

Carlos nods sipping his chocolate.

"Is that with Peter Cushing?"

Tanya puts the magazine back on the coffee table.

"No, it's with Christopher Lee."

Carlos's eyes light up like a child with a new toy.

"Oh I like Christopher Lee; he was a great, yeah let's put that one on. Anyway, we know the ending in the Titanic—everyone dies."

Tanya laughs.

Carlos laughs too.

"What are you laughing at?"

Tanya kisses Carlos.

"I think you will find they all die in this one too at the end."

"Damn Tanya, now you've gone and spoiled it."

Carlos laughs and switches on the TV with the remote control.

They lounge back on the sofa together and the opening credits are already rolling.

Carlos looks at Tanya.

"This is going to be good."

Tanya looks surprised.

"You haven't seen this before?"

"Sure I have, that's how I know, oh by the way, they do not all die in the end!"

***

The clock on the tower of St John's Church was shining bright showing the time. Larry checks his wristwatch against the church clock – 11:45 pm.

"Well I knew it was late but, oh well."

Larry stops and swings his shovel over his shoulder as he bends down and picks up an old copy of The Cornish Times.

"The rubbish that blows in here, sweet wrappers, newspapers, I don't know."

Larry has been the ground man and caretaker of St John's for twenty two years and has got to know the locals in the village very well.

Larry being quite a character but not really the sharpest knife in the draw at times, is a loveable chap, or so they say. Although only in his early fifties, he still could be mistaken for late forties with a good clean up. He is six feet tall and slim with greying hair in need of a wash, dirty nails and a moustache that needs a trim.

"Time to put this lot in the van and head on home."

Often Larry would chat away to himself while he's working or sing a little song.

He always has a smile and a tale to tell wherever he goes and with whomever he meets.

In the churchyard, the wind continues to howl through the trees. Larry looks up to the trees.

"Yes, I know you're waking up, blowing old leaves all over my freshly cleaned up graves. Oh well, that'll give me something to do when morning breaks."

Larry swings the shovel back around and sticks it into the fresh soil of the grave, then puts the old newspaper in the black bag on the floor.

Picking up the bag, Larry shivers.

Larry shakes his head he chuckles to himself.

"Sleep tight."

He throws the bin into his wheelbarrow and walks off down the path towards the gated entrance of the churchyard.

The paths were clean and well kept, the grass was in perfect condition.

The railings around the graveyard were in need of a lick of paint and the gate needs oiling but that was on his list of things to do.

The wind howled and blew across the graveyard as Larry reached his van.

A flower blew in the wind onto the grave and stopped when it hit Larry's shovel.

The dirt on the grave moves and shudders, the flower begins to decompose and die.

Just along the path outside the church is a large industrial bin where Larry throws his rubbish. He heads back to the van and as he opens the doors, they creak.

"What is it with doors?"

Larry puts the barrow in the back of the van along with endless tools and ropes and reels of wire and sacks scattered in no particular order all over the place. The light in the back flickers on and off.

Larry shakes his head.

"That's another couple of jobs to do. Oil the gates and these doors and fix the light. Never ending this job is. Work, work, work and more bloody work, oh well, that's life I suppose."

The soil continued to shudder and fresh soil rolled to the sides. The shovel fell to the side of the grave, and then everything stopped, just silence.

Then bang. The soil flew into the air and the lid from the coffin followed like an explosion.

Chapter Two

Larry gets into his old Ford van and closes the door. He turns on the engine and its starts the first time.

Larry has had this van from new and it is now twelve years old and in need of some serious work but it does the job for now and on his small wage he has no choice but just to keep repairing it until it finally dies.

He buckles up and pulls out onto the road.

Larry puts on his window wipers to clear the condensation from the window screen caused by the Cornish evening air. Patchy fog is a regular occurrence on these parts of the village and tonight was no exception.

The winding roads can be dangerous at night if you don't know where you are driving, as most of the lanes and roads are not lit up at all and you just rely on your head lamps. But Larry knows them like the back of his hand.

The tall trees bend over the narrow lanes almost making part of the road seem like a tunnel. At night, the smell of wild flowers and grass fill the air and trails off into the night sky.

Larry turns a corner and there is thick fog just as he had expected so he slows down to a steady twenty-three miles per hour. Through the fog, he is sure he could see a figure of a person, he couldn't quite make it out so he slows right down and peeps his horn just for precaution. Larry didn't want to knock anyone over. It's bad enough squashing a rabbit or hare or the occasional stray cat that darts across the road.

This has happened to Larry not so long back and the thud of the cat banging under the van still remains as clear as day to him. So, it's always best to be on the safe side and take the necessary precaution just in case.

He was now travelling at ten miles per hour and realises it is a young woman standing in the road.

The girl couldn't have been more than thirty-five years old and had long dark hair which was gently moving with the cool breeze of the night. Her face was pale and her eyes were dark. Larry could only just see the whites of her eyes as they were shadowed by her fringe. Her cheekbones were chiselled and lips dark red and perfectly formed.

Larry pulled over and stopped the van. He wound down his window to speak with the young girl.

"You'll get knocked over standing there. Are you OK?"

The girl just stands there looking at Larry.

"Are you OK, my dear?"

No answer.

"Where are you from?"

The girl tilts her head slightly and almost moves her lips to smile.

"Not far from here."

"Hop in. I can drop you off if you like."

The young girl nods, she seems to thank him with a slow blink of her eyes; if he wasn't so tired he would have probably thought he was being seduced by her eyes.

"It's too cold to be out late at night dressed like that."

The young girl just stares at Larry.

"Have you been walking in your sleep?"

She just shrugs her shoulders and then turns her head and looks out of the window in the door.

"OK well, never mind, let's just see if we can get you home."

Larry slowly pulls back out onto the road and drives into the dense fog. In seconds, his taillights disappear into the foggy night.

Even though Larry knew these winding roads like the back of his hand, he still was driving much slower than usual especially now he has a passenger to look after. Up ahead a bright light seemed to be shining directly at him.

"What's all this?"

Larry slowed down as he approached the light. Getting closer he realised it was a torch being shone at his window screen.

Larry stops his van. A figure of a man walks through the fog towards them. He realised it was a policeman and as he got closer he recognised it to be Sergeant Pike. Larry winds down his window.

Sergeant Pike stoops down and looks into the van window. In his broad Cornish accent, he smiles.

"Good evening, Larry."

The fog was thinning out and Larry could make out a police car and also an ambulance ahead.

"Evening Sergeant, what's the problem?"

"Fatality."

"Oh dear, was it an accident?"

"I don't know, I just found the body lying there."

Larry blows his nose.

"It's Susan."

"Susan?"

"Susan Moorcroft from the post office."

Larry gasps and leans back in his seat for a second.

"Oh no, poor girl … it's very strange, that's three in a week; I shall be running out of space to put them all."

Sergeant Pike chuckles at Larry's remark.

"You haven't lost your sense of humour, Larry."

"Well there's too much heartache in the world, you got to keep your spirits up. Anyway, I better go I need to drop…"

Larry turns and notices the young girl has disappeared. Larry turns and stares up at Sergeant Pike in disbelief.

"Are you OK?"

Larry stumbles over his words and can't quite understand what has just happened.

"I… I think I need to sleep; it's been a long day."

"Drive carefully now. It's a bit patchy tonight with this fog."

Sergeant Pike stands back and taps the top of Larry van. Larry pulls away off into the fog.

***

Susan Moorcroft was only in her late twenties. She was a pretty, blonde with big blue eyes and had worked at the post office since she left college. Susan was an only child and both her parents live abroad. Her only living relative is her aunt who is disabled and lives in the village.

21

Tonight she lay face up in the body bag; all pale, even her lips were as pale as her cheeks. The paramedic gently closes her eyes with his fingers before zipping up the bag.

Sergeant Pike watches the paramedics move the body into the ambulance.

***

Larry continues to drive down the narrow lanes of this Cornish coast in and out of patchy fog chatting away to himself under his breath.

"I don't know what this place is coming to."

Thick fog surrounding his van so he slows down as he turns the corner.

The fog clears for a bit and on the side of the road he notices a girl.

"What's this?"

He pulls over next to the girl and it soon becomes apparent that it's the same girl he had met earlier who mysteriously disappeared from his van.

Was he dreaming? Did he dream the whole thing or was it déjà vu?

Everything was going through his mind even to the point of thinking was he going a little crazy.

Without Larry uttering a single word the girl walks straight over to the van and opens the door then gets in.

Larry looks completely stunned.

"You don't mind if I…?"

Larry cuts in.

"What happened to you? How did you…"

The girl begins to giggle.

"Sorry? I haven't seen you before. I would remember a handsome man like you."

"You're lost? That's what you said…"

The girl continues to laugh and Larry is starting to feel somewhat uneasy about things.

"Lost? Not lost. No, just looking for some company, are you single?"

Larry looks directly into her eyes. They are black as night and lips as red as a rose petal. Larry felt almost hypnotised by her but couldn't understand why.

His mind was telling him to kick her out but something else was telling him not to. What was this magnetic charm she had over him? What was it?

"Well yes I am, and too old for you. But that's…"

The girl cuts Larry off.

"Too old for me. You don't know how old I am. I just might look good for my age."

"No, I'm sure I am older than you. Shall…"

The girl cuts Larry off again mid-sentence.

"Good, we can go back to yours then, I can show you a good time."

Larry plucks up courage and grabs hold of the steering wheel with both hands.

"Look here, if you're after money I don't get paid enough to pay for…"

The girl stares at Larry for a few seconds then smirks. She wipes her top teeth seductively with her tongue.

"I'm not a prostitute, don't worry. Just lonely, looking for some company, that's all."

"Oh well, that's OK then. I just didn't want you to think… anyway."

Larry pulls away and continues to drive; this time he knows where he is going. Straight home as fast as he can. Offers don't come that often for Larry and he isn't going to miss an opportunity with a beautiful, young and feisty girl.

He could have his wicked way and she could be gone by the morning and no one need even know.

She is a stranger in town. So, yes, definitely no one would even find out.

As Larry is concentrating and driving through the foggy lanes the girl begins to rub her hand up and down Larry's leg and then up to his crotch. She has a menacing look in her eyes as she licks her lips.

Larry gulps back saliva.

"You shouldn't do that while I'm driving, it's really foggy down these lanes. I could have an accident."

"Do you have children?"

Larry feels himself getting an erection.

"No."

"Do you want children?"

She continues to rub his crotch feeling his bulge and gently squeezing around his balls.

"That's a strange question, and a bit random, isn't it?"

"Is it?"

Larry still feels uneasy and tries not looking at the girl partly because of being embarrassed and the other he needs to keep his eyes on the road as much as possible. And also he doesn't want to let an opportunity like this pass him by.

***

The fog seems to have lifted, well not as thick anyhow. They pass several small houses and cottages and Larry slows down and checks his wrist watch, the time is now 12:57.

"Almost one o'clock."

The girl smiles at Larry.

"Yes, but the night is young."

Larry turns a corner and slows down and almost immediately turns into a small drive. He stops the van.

Larry takes off his seat belt.

"One sec."

Larry opens the van door and walks up to a large white garage door with a rusty handle. He pulls the handle back and the garage door swings up high and folds into the roof of the garage. A dim yellow light turns on revealing several old bikes, one hanging on the wall. There is a long wooden bench filled up with tools. Most of the garage is piled up with junk that he has probably collected over a number of years – there is even an old doll's pram in one corner.

Larry gets back into the van and shuts the door.

"If you get out while I park the van."

This command made sense as there was very little room if any to even open the passenger door when parked in the garage. In fact, there was only just enough room for Larry to get out and even then he couldn't open his door fully.

Larry locks the van and then shuts down the garage door and locks it. He tests the handle to make sure it is firmly locked then gestures to the girl towards the front door.

It is a small house made of local stone and brick. The windows were narrow and the front door was hidden behind a cute little porch with flower baskets on either side. There are flower beds aplenty and rose bushes in all four corners.

There are even a few gnomes taken directly from the seven dwarfs, keeping watch over the house.

Larry walks up to the porch and swings his front door keys around his finger then stops and looks at the girl.

"Do you know we have travelled for almost fifteen minutes and I still don't know your name?"

The girl just is about to speak when Larry finishes abruptly.

"No, don't tell me, I think it's more of a mystery, yes, it's like one of those films where you never quite know how it will end but keeps you guessing, and I think it's quite romantic as well."

"You do?"

Larry fumbles with the key in the shaded porch for the keyhole then unlocks the door.

***

In the churchyard, there is complete silence, not even an owl tooting and not even a bird rustling in the trees.

Just complete silence, only the dead sleeping in their coffins and the birds sleeping in their nests.

The church is lit by the full moon and the clock reads ten past one in the morning.

The old wooden door leading down to the crypt seems to have a haze on the step like steam from a kettle.

The haze is getting thicker and mist seeps from beneath the door, rising up above the door clinging to and climbing up the stone church wall.

***

The young girl is in bed with Larry, they are kissing passionately while Larry's right hand rubs gently up and down the side of the girl's body, even the hard skin on Larry's hand brushing up and over the girls erect nipple makes her murmur in ecstasy.

Larry's hard penis is gently massaging the lips of her vulva as he motions his body like the waves of the ocean gently up and down teasing her vagina with the tip of his penis.

The girl bites her lip as Larry enters her as she gasps in ecstasy. Larry pushes his penis in deep and hard.

She bends her legs as he thrusts hard and can feel his scrotum gently banging against her anus.

Her eyes roll into the back of her head as she licks her lips. When Larry kisses her neck, he can taste the salty sweat.

They change position and the girl sits down on Larry riding him like a wild animal. The moonlight is shining through the window, and Larry has his eyes closed enjoying every minute, every second, wondering how long he can hold back before he explodes and fills her with his hot white cum.

As she rides Larry, up and down, the sweat is running down her back and into the crack of her buttocks.

Two bats hover at the window, the girl watches them for a while before they fly off.

Larry opens his eyes.

"I'm going to cum."

She throws back her head and screams.

Chapter Three

Suddenly Larry jumps in his bed as the alarm clock rings. Eight o'clock in the morning and the sun is rising outside. The rays of the morning sun always hit the bedroom at this time of the morning, as they break through the mass of trees in the field out the back of the house. The field stretches as far as the eye can see on a clear day.

There is still a smell of stale sex, musty and tangy.

A smell Larry hasn't smelt in a long, long time, which is why it was so noticeable on this bright morning in September.

Larry reaches for his wrist watch that always lies on his side cabinet, next to the bed where the tissues and alarm clock sit, and also a small coaster with tea stained rings.

He then realises the girl has gone. His mysterious girl, that lady of the night, had disappeared once more.

The more he thought about it the more he realised it must have been the same person he had picked up before just down the road from the accident.

"Oh my God, the accident!"

His mind was turning over and over he just couldn't get that girl out from his mind. She had infected his head, his mind, taken advantage of his body and his soul.

What did she want, who was she, and why hadn't he seen her before? Larry could have kicked himself. Under his breath he began to mumble.

"You and your 'no don't tell me your name.' I like a mystery, a fantasy. Well you got that alright."

Larry swings around out of the bed completely naked. Scratch marks run down the length of his back. He grabs a fresh towel from a draw in the cupboard and heads of to the shower. On the landing, Larry shouts down the stairs.

"Hello, are you downstairs?"

Larry waits for an answer knowing really that there wouldn't be one. There was nothing, not a sound.

Larry opens the bathroom door and enters.

The bathroom was quite a size, with a long bath and a separate show cubical. Not like the old shower over the bath job. Everything was white, the tiles, the toilet, the bath and the shower – everything gleaming white.

Clearly, Larry liked white as even the flannels and towels all matched in white.

Larry stepped inside the shower and turned on the tap.

Hot steaming water poured out as Larry lathered himself all over with coconut shower gel.

***

Larry was sure he had a whiff of the girl as he was driving into town in his van. He kept checking the passenger seat just in case his mysterious girl appeared again.

It was a lovely morning and the sun was shining and the sky was a lovely pale blue. It always turns out nice after a bit of fog, Larry has always been fascinated by the weather and checks on the weather every morning. Larry always likes to know because when you're in his line of work gravedigging or gardening in the graveyard you need to know in advance if it's going to be a rainy day or if it's going to be a sharp frost or even snow – not that it snows too much in Cornwall.

Larry pulls into the village and parks up the van outside the post office.

He gets out and locks the van and then walks down the street, deep in thought.

The accident flashes through his mind. The foggy night, and the mysterious girl keeps dominating his thoughts – but why? The post office, Sergeant Pike and the paramedics all keep pounding in his head as he walks through the quiet village street.

Sally's bicycle bell rings loud in his ears and he nearly jumps out of his skin.

"Oh, Larry, I'm sorry, did I make you jump, my lovely?"

Sally swings her leg over the bicycle seat and pulls the stand out with her pointed brown shoes – not really practical for riding but Sally's favourite pair – that go with her brown and yellow dress. An acquired taste but nevertheless, Sally seams to pull off anything she puts on with her slim size ten figure and red hair.

"It's OK."

"You're late this morning. Are you sure you're OK?"

Sally was a caring person working as a home help, looking after the elderly. And being in her early thirties, she had a kind of girlish charm still. The old people seemed to love her, wanting to mother her.

"Yes, I had a bit of a strange night."

"Don't tell me you were swept off your feet by a beautiful woman and she kept you up all night?"

"Well, I… I…"

Larry became all flustered.

"I'm just messing with you."

"I seemed to have slept really heavily. But do you know I don't feel I have slept at all. I know that doesn't make any sense but that's exactly how I feel."

Sally looks at Larry all seriously.

"Change is coming, that's what that is. Well that's what my mum always says anyhow."

"Now don't you go all strange on me, there's enough strange things going on around here without you adding to them all."

"Oh never mind me, Larry."

"I'm just a bit jittery what with everything that's going on."

Sally gets back on her bike oblivious to Larry's mutterings.

"I better get off now and get the newspaper and a few bits for Miss Moorcroft."

Larry grabs Sally's arm.

"Miss Moorcroft? How is she coping after Susan's accident?"

Sally looks shocked.

"Accident! What accident? When?"

"Oh you haven't heard yet, of course you wouldn't, it was only last night."

Sally can tell by Larry's face it was serious and begins to look worried.

"Why, what happened?"

Larry holds Sally's hand; it is the only way he can think of to comfort her. He knows the news is going to be a big shock as she knows the family very well.

"Susan's body was found in the lane close to the graveyard. I was driving home when they found her."

"Oh my God that's terrible. Who found her? Did they say what had happened?"

Larry shakes his head; he can see tears in Sally's eyes.

"They didn't say. The police found the body, I presume. They were there when I drove home, it was really late."

Sally wipes a tear with her fingers that ran down and rested on her cheek.

"I better get off and make sure Miss Moorcroft is OK."

Larry comforts her best he can by rubbing her shoulder.

"OK, my lovely, give her my love."

Sally gets back on her bike, then just before she moves away she suddenly stops.

"Oh, Larry before I dash, I went to put some flowers on Granny's grave and I nearly went down that open grave. You should cover the hole up."

Larry looks extremely puzzled; he stands quiet for a second.

"Open grave?" He questions as he steps backwards. "There aren't any open graves."

Sally could see he really was sure about what he was saying but she knew differently.

"There is, Larry. I should know, I nearly ended up at the bottom of the hole. It's dangerous, you should put something over it."

As Sally rides off, Larry shakes his head and looks at his watch looking completely baffled.

10:20 am and he still hadn't started work. A normal day for Larry is an 8 am start but today just didn't feel right.

After a full day of odd jobs from oiling his van doors to cutting the church grass, the day was moving fast.

Larry looked up at the sky, it was beginning to darken as the clouds got thicker and what sunlight they had that day just disappeared. The church clock was at 5:35 pm when Larry suddenly remembered the grave!

Larry's maintenance shed was close by so he wandered over and rummaged for his keys amongst old tissues in his pocket. He unlocked the shed and removed a large sheet of wood which he balanced on his wheel barrow, then headed off towards the grave.

Larry was a dab hand at balancing stuff on this barrow. Many a time he had transported old coffins and bits of wood or items that people had just dumped close to the graveyard and sometimes even inside the graveyard.

Larry reached the grave and looked over into the hole.

The coffin was still there, the lid was nowhere to be seen and the coffin was empty.

How could this be? Who on earth would want to remove a body from a grave? All these questions kept on repeating and flashing through Larry's head. Larry placed the large wooden board over the hole then headed back to the shed.

Chapter Four

The sea is rough tonight on the Cornish coast. The waves are getting higher with every rush towards the rocks scattered about the coast line. Storms are no stranger to these Cornish shores and some people even look forward to them, watching them, relishing in the excitement of seeing the mighty waves; some ten, some twenty or thirty feet high, some even higher. These storms have shaped the Cornish coastline over the years and tonight there is another blowing in, moving the water, angry, fast and furious towards the rocks.

Rumbling of thunder can be heard rolling across the Atlantic Ocean. A flash of lightening lights up the whole sky, silhouetting the gulls flying high, fleeing to a distant place, a tree, a nest. Anywhere so they can rest their wings out from the storm.

The lighthouse in the distance looks like a toy perched upon a rock. The waves are pounding causing white foam to fly up high into the sky.

The radio room in the lighthouse was fairly old and was in need of an update. The equipment had been there since the early fifties and still worked perfectly but really should have been updated forty years ago.

Jack was watching through the window in the radio room, watching the storm while Freddy sat at the table trying to build a house from playing cards.

"It's going to be a rough one, Freddy boy."

Jack always called Freddy 'boy' because he was only thirty two years old and Jack, being fifty four, treated him like a son. Freddy was a simple lad, some would describe him as backward but he was a good person who was always eager to help. He had worked at the lighthouse since he was a young boy, which is another reason why they still refer to him as boy.

Jack on the other hand likes to have a moan and often is referred to as doom and gloom; he loves a good storm – the bigger the better.

The thunder still frightens Freddy but Jack loves being frightened and finds it amusing when Freddy jumps. Jack always knows when Freddy is nervous or frightened because he starts to stammer.

"Looks like it… Err, Jack, fancy a game of cards later?"

Jack takes a second to think about it.

"Maybe."

"Great."

Jack sits down at the table opposite Freddy.

Freddy tells Jack quite excitedly.

"George will be over tonight?"

"With that damn dog?"

Jack doesn't like George's dog. In fact, he doesn't like dogs at all.

"Yes, with the dog. He's a good dog; he's company for him."

George lives alone with his dog and after his wife died, he has wrapped himself up with work at the lighthouse and refuses to retire even though he is almost sixty-nine-years-old.

Jack gets up from the table and heads on over to the refrigerator then opens the door and looks inside, there are cans of beer and some margarine in a tub and some jam.

"It's a good job Rusty can hear 'cause George's hearing is getting worse by the day."

Freddy leans around on the chair to face Jack.

"I told him to get a deaf aid; he says it makes his ear itch!"

Jack chuckles and smiles. He then bangs down a bottle of un-opened beer on the table.

"Beer?"

"Why not! Thanks, you got any nuts over there?"

Jack smiles and pulls a face with his tongue hanging out the side of his mouth as he grabs his crotch and squeezes it close to Freddy. "Only these. Will they do?"

Freddy moves back and pushes Jack away.

"Pervert."

Jack laughs and holds up the margarine.

"I'll tell you what we do need though."

Freddy looks at the margarine.

"What? Margarine?"

Jack turns towards the bread bin and holds up a mouldy loaf.

"Bread!"

Freddy looks over to the freezer in the corner of the room, small and a little rusty in places but still works perfectly.

"Have you checked the freezer, Jack?"

Jack spins on one foot in the direction of the freezer pointing his fingers out like two guns, this makes Freddy smile. Jack opens the freezer and bends down looking in the freezer and spots a loaf of bread.

"Bingo."

***

The lightning flashes, almost blinding Carlos as it seems to bounce of his window screen as he drives home from work.

The rain is pounding down onto the window screen and the window washers can hardly keep up. The visibility is practically zero and there is very little lighting down these winding country roads.

These Cornish roads can be lethal when bad weather hits, especially a storm like tonight. Carlos desperately waits for the next lightening flash so he can see what's ahead of him. He is now barely driving at twenty miles an hour, sometimes less. Fortunately Carlos' jeep holds the road pretty well and on a straight stretch of road he can put his foot down slightly. The wheels tear through the puddles, showering the side of the jeep with muddy water and any animal that is within reach.

In his brad American accent, he shouts out loudly,

"OK, let's have some music!"

He turns on the player and country music blares out.

"Yahoooo! That's more like it, now we're cooking on gas."

Carlos sings along as best as he can, almost drowning out the song.

***

Tanya is busy baking in the kitchen waiting for Carlos to get home from work. She opens the oven door and pulls out the tray with her bright pink oven gloves. She puts the tray on the large wooden table and carefully empties the tray on to cooling racks.

She checks outside looking through the kitchen window. The rain is still heavy and the storm is still raging outside.

Lewis runs into the kitchen and smells the cake in the air, his eyes light up.

"Wow, can I have a bit?"

"Not yet, wait until it's cooled down and I have finished it off."

Lewis was only twelve years old coming up for thirteen in just a couple of months. He was a bright kid and obsessed with horror movies. His bedroom was covered in posters and models and books from monster movies from the thirties right up to present day.

He was good at school and had good grades so Carlos and Tanya weren't too worried about his hobby; in fact, they just thought he would one day grow out of it.

Tanya puts three plates on the dining table then moves the cooling rack with the cake onto the worktop and finishes laying the table.

Lewis looks at the three plates then looks up at his mum.

"I'm not that hungry. And I've got to study."

"So you won't want dinner then?"

"Not really, I'll get a sandwich later with my bit of cake."

Lewis looks up at his mum with his big brown eyes, he gets them from his dad's side of the family; in fact, Lewis takes after his dad in a lot of ways he has that lovely naturally tanned skin like his dad. That was the Latin side of the family.

Tanya smiles and rubs the top of his hair and messes it up.

"Go on then."

Lewis looks up with those big brown eyes and smiles.

"Sorry, Mum."

"It's OK, go on with you."

"Well, I have got my exam next week."

"I know. I'll dish you a plate up and you can warm it in the microwave. You can't live on sandwiches and cake."

"Thanks Mum, I love you."

Tanya's heart always melts when she hears her little boy telling her he loves her, she watches Lewis run out of the kitchen then she turns and walks over to the sink smiling to herself.

**

Carlos pulls up into the drive; he jumps out as quickly as he can, opens up the back door of the jeep and grabs his bag and coat, then slams the door shut and locks it.

Tanya hears the backdoor close while she is at the sink washing up. She calls out.

"Take your boots off."

Carlos calls back.

"Taking them off."

Carlos walks up to Tanya in the kitchen while she is at the sink washing up. He puts his arms around her and kisses her neck. Tanya turns her head and kisses Carlos on his lips.

"Did you have a good day?"

"Oh yes."

Carlos turns and slaps Tanya's bottom gently.

"I have some good news."

Tanya turns around and takes off her pink marigolds as if she means business. Carlos looks over and spots the cake, "Now that smells good."

"It isn't finished yet."

Carlos is as bad as Lewis for cake and all things sweet; Tanya always tells him he is like a big kid.

"So, what news?"

"Ah yes, well, I won't be driving those big water tanks around much longer."

Tanya looks puzzled.

"Oh?"

"They have given me a desk job."

Tanya gets annoyed, "Well this is terrible news and after all the years you have worked for them and they treat you like this. I suppose it will be less money too?"

Carlos smiles.

"Calm down babe, calm down."

"How do you expect me to react?"

"I've been promoted to management."

Tanya's face lights up; she rushes over and hugs Carlos really tightly.

"Well why didn't you say, that's fantastic news darling."

"You didn't give me much chance to be honest now, did you?"

"I'm sorry."

"Oh, and I got a big pay rise."

"That's brilliant darling."

"I even get my name on a door."

They both laugh out loud.

"It just gets better and better."

They both continue to laugh. Carlos sits down at the table and Tanya sits on his lap with her arms around his neck. She kisses him on the tip of his nose which makes Carlos blink in a kind of cute way that always makes Tanya laugh.

"So does that mean we will be able to have a holiday now?"

Carlos nods then kisses Tanya back on the nose.

"Oh yes, and you can choose."

"Now that sounds good to me."

"Not too expensive though. Where is Lewis?"

Tanya gestures with her head.

"He's upstairs studying he has an exam next week. Dinner will be ready in about 20 minutes, so you can lay the table for me while you're here. Only two places, Lewis is eating later when he has finished his studying."

Carlos gives Tanya another peck on the nose.

"OK, just let me get out of these dirty overalls and have a quick shower then I can lay the table."

"Oh don't worry I'll do it, you go and have your shower."

Tanya kisses Carlos.

"You never know I might even surprise you and jump in with you."

Chapter Five

The crypt in Saint John's Church hasn't been used for decades. It is dark and damp.

The wooden door is as old as the church. The lock is brown and black with rust and hasn't been opened in years.

Inside the crypt there is a small light coming from a long and narrow broken stained-glass window, covered in rusty wire mesh with a coating of spider webs and dust that has collected over the years.

The one thing this crypt isn't short of is spiders and rats – an ideal breeding ground for such creatures.

There is a broken tomb with a coffin lying inside.

In the coffin lays the girl. The girl that Larry picked up on his journey back from work; she is still as the night.

Her stomach looks swollen; she is pregnant and carrying Larry's baby.

But so soon, how could this be. This girl is a breeder and a vampire, her only needs are to multiply, to breed, to drink blood and to kill.

There is a creak in the crypt, a noise from deep inside, way back in the dark.

The girl's eyes open. They are blood red.

Carlos is holding Tanya's hand across the dinner table which is situated in the kitchen. They are both looking into each other's eyes still clearly very much in love.

The dirty dinner plates are piled up and left on the side along with the saucepans, all ready to be washed in the sink.

Tanya refused to have a dishwasher and prefers the old hand washing method, so they made a decision to take it in turns washing up.

Tonight, it is Tanya's turn, but after a good meal like tonight's meat pie and potatoes, they like to sit and chat and relax with a nice hot cup of tea.

Carlos is more of a coffee drinker in the day but tea in the morning and in the evening unless it's wine or a beer.

Tanya on the other hand is a wine drinker or occasionally she will partake in a cheeky gin and tonic of an evening.

Carlos shakes his head and closes his eyes.

"Jamaica will be too hot."

"Really?"

"Yep."

"How about Australia?"

"Maybe, but I think could still be too hot."

"Oh, you're impossible."

Carlos laughs.

While they discuss what holiday destination they prefer, mist slowly seeps in from outside and under the back door and creeps up the wall and crawls across the ceiling where it settles.

Tanya and Carlos are still throwing destinations back and forth trying to decide which one is best for them, oblivious to the mist settling above their heads.

The mist forms into the vampire girl from the crypt.

"Canada! What about Canada?"

Carlos is still in disagreement with nearly all of Tanya's suggestions.

"Why not Spain?"

Tanya crosses her arms, she is getting a little annoyed and is not sure if Carlos is being awkward or just playing with her.

"Everyone goes to Spain."

"Florida, I've not been back since we met?"

Tanya met Carlos while on holiday in Florida back in 1988 and fell desperately in love. They wrote and travelled back and forth until Tanya accepted his hand in marriage.

They married in Cyprus Gardens in Florida and lived there for a number of years until Tanya's dad got sick. So they relocated back to Cornwall, Tanya's hometown, until her father passed on.

"Oh I know, what about Brazil?"

"Oh, I see. Because the men are hot in Brazil!"

"No, not at all. I already have a hot man."

Carlos gets up.

"Come here."

Tanya gets up and he pulls her close and kisses her.

"Florida it is then."

The vampire leaps from the ceiling and lands beside Tanya and Carlos, she snarls like an animal, she has sharp canine fangs and her eyes are blood red.

They are both in shock but Tanya manages to scream. The vampire knocks her across the room and against the wall cabinet, banging her head with such force, knocking her unconscious.

***

Lewis is busy studying when he hears his mum scream and then a loud bang. He jumps up and stops to listen but there is silence. He decides to check out if everything is OK. He calls down over the landing.

"Mum, are you OK?"

There is no answer so Lewis slowly moves down the stairs the cottage is old and the stairs creak, so it is very hard not to make a noise. At the bottom of the stairs he stops.

He knows something is up, his body is telling him, his sixth sense is telling him. *Burglars*, he thinks, *I need to prepare myself. I need something, a baseball bat. Yes, that's it, I need a bat.* The bat was upstairs and he didn't want to climb up again in case they hear. He looks around and the only thing he can find is an umbrella. That should be OK, it's better than nothing, at least it has a sharp point on the end. Lewis begins to tremble inside; the nerves are kicking in as he approaches the kitchen door. He slowly looks around the door and freezes with fright.

His dad is standing still, staring into space as if he was in a trance, his mum is lying across the floor and a strange woman is undoing his dad's shirt. The woman senses Lewis at the door and turns her head and opens her blood red eyes and hisses, the kitchen door slams shut in Lewis's face.

Lewis runs up the stairs as fast as he can and runs into his bedroom and shuts the door and locks it. He stands with his back against the door.

There are tears in his eyes, his heart pounding extremely fast, breathless and white as a sheet wondering what on earth he had just seen. He closes his eyes and tries to control his breathing. Knowing he is helpless, a tear rolls down the side of his face. A few seconds pass and he opens his eyes, and the first thing he sees is a poster of Christopher Lee as Dracula. Fangs and bloodshot eyes staring straight at him. But this time only on paper.

Chapter Six

The moon is surprisingly large tonight. The clouds are still in the sky, not as thick but moving quite fast across the Cornish sky.

The storm has moved on to some other place or just exhausted itself until there was nothing left.

The lighthouse casts its beam of light across the cold Atlantic sea, cutting through the sea mist and foggy Cornish shoreline.

Three large bats fly across the night sky silhouetted by the moon, heading towards the lighthouse.

The bats land on the lighthouse wall and begin to change. They seem to stretch and change shape. All three doing the exact same thing. They are changing, morphing into three girls snarling like animals in the moonlight.

They crawl down the wall until they reach the bottom.

***

Jack, Freddy and George are playing a game of cards at the table in the radio room. They all have bottles of beer and a couple of bags of crisps are screwed up next to the bin, on the floor, where they have been thrown but missed.

Rusty, George's dog, begins to bark. They all stop playing cards and look over to Rusty.

George puts his hand down and wriggles his fingers to summon his dog.

"What's up boy, you've been out once."

Rusty comes over and tugs at George's hand then heads back over to the door where he continues to bark.

Jack looks over to his empty food bowl.

"Maybe he wants some food, he might be hungry."

"He's not long been fed Jack; I don't know what's up with him. It's not like him to be like this."

Rusty was scraping at the door barking louder and louder.

He then stops and begins to whimper at the door.

Freddy turns in his seat to look at Rusty and throws him a crisp. Rusty normally loves crisps but tonight he wasn't taking interest in anything. He was acting really strange.

Normally he would lie down and sleep or give you kisses and want to sit on your lap, just a normal Yorkshire terrier really. But tonight, George couldn't make out what was up with him.

"Well something is up, he wants to go out."

"Maybe you're right Fred. Go on boy, go and see."

George opens up the door and Rusty runs down the spiral staircase.

At the bottom of the stairs, the three vampires stand in almost darkness, apart from a small lamp on the wall lighting up their pale gaunt features.

They hear Rusty barking as he runs down the stairs.

One of the girls immediately starts to transform. She collapses to the floor on all fours. Her body starts jerking and twisting, morphing into the shape of a wolf. Her spine protruding under her skin, her jaw pushes forward stretching her mouth. Its fangs grow long and sharp and begin to snap and snarl at the air. Hair quickly covers the torso.

As Rusty reaches the bottom of the stairs he stops barking, as he sees the wolf staring snarling at him. Rusty slowly backs off whimpering.

George is standing at the slightly open door listening for Rusty. There is silence.

"He must have wanted a pee, he's all quiet now."

Jack opens the fridge.

"Another beer anyone?"

Everyone agrees to that in one big yes please, probably a stupid question really, three men playing cards with nothing much else to do, other than listen for SOS signals or watch the storms or play cards. So, beer is always a welcome option for these chaps.

"George, come and sit down."

Freddy pulls out George's chair at the table.

Jack returns with three bottles of ale, he opens them at the table and hands them out, then sits down. Jack holds up his bottle.

"Cheers everyone, health, happiness and I hope I win the next round of cards."

They all laugh.

"Right, who's going to deal?"

"You can, Jack."

Jack notices that Freddy keeps looking at the door.

"What's up boy?"

"Rusty's been a while."

George pats Freddy on the back.

"Probably found a cat."

Jack sharply answers back.

"Where's he going to find a cat, we're in a lighthouse not a bloody village?"

George swigs his beer and agrees with a nod.

"He's got a point."

The room is quite dark and only a few small lights are scattered around the walls some of them are turned off. A light hanging from a long cord over the table, lights up the card game and their bottles of beer.

The door opens very slowly, no one notices as they are all busy playing cards and drinking and joking. The three vampire girls crawl in slowly and move to the corner where it is in complete darkness. They crawl up the wall and on to the ceiling then wait and watch.

The vampires all look at each other then all at once they leap down and grab Freddy, George and Jack by the throats.

The vampire girl who has hold of Jack is pregnant and is showing slightly. She is the same girl that seduced Larry only last night. She lifts Jack a few inches of the ground like a rag doll. She turns her head and looks around at Freddy and George and then back at the girls. She snarls.

"Time for feeding."

They all tip the heads back in unison and sink their fangs deep into the jugular veins of these helpless men. They let go, only holding onto their victims by their teeth and with a stretch of their arms they all begin to change into giant bats rising up, still holding each of the men by their teeth, drinking and draining the blood, the life and souls from their useless bodies. Their faces getting paler, their lips bluer until their eyes roll into the back of their heads. One by one they each drop the empty bodies to the floor.

Chapter Seven

Lewis is sitting on the bed, putting his trainers on as fast as he can sweating in total panic, he jumps up from the bed and opens his wardrobe and pulls out a blue puffer jacket and puts it on. He grabs his baseball bat from under his bed.

He unlocks the bedroom door then panics again and locks it back up; he turns his back to the door then slides down and puts his head in his hands. He bangs his hand on his head in frustration; he is terrified. He jumps back up and runs to the window. Maybe the burglars have a car.

Lewis was thinking out loud.

"Maybe I can write the car registration number down."

Lewis looks out the window at the evening and there is nothing, just an empty road and across the road, the field that backs onto St John's church. Nothing, nothing but grass trees, bushes and grave stones.

***

Carlos is lying on the kitchen floor on his back. The vampire girl is sitting on him, riding him in ecstasy, up and down, with motions fast and hard, her long tongue rolling around her lips and across her long sharp fangs. Her eyes open fierce and bloodshot, her hair is long blond and messy and somewhat dirty.

Tanya lay still in the corner of the room, her eyes begin to flutter and her vision is somewhat blurry. Her eyes begin to focus as the vampire screams out in ecstasy. Immediately the vampire turns her head to look at Tanya as if she had sensed her waking up. She climbed of Carlos leaving him lying in a trance. She crawls over to Tanya and pulls Tanya's head to her breasts and strokes her hair like a mother with a baby.

The girl's face is pretty: she is blond, her eyes are blue, she is beautiful. She smiles at Tanya then tilts her head back, her face changes into that gruesome evil monster she was before. Her eyes are blood red and her fangs long and sharp, pulling Tanya's head back by her hair, she sinks her fangs into her throat then in one quick movement she tips her head back, Tanya's blood running from the vampire's mouth.

Tanya lay on the floor once more this time in a trance drained of blood and weak. The vampire stands up wipes her mouth on the back of her hand.

***

Lewis is still watching out his bedroom window, thinking, frightened, wondering what to do. Then suddenly he notices the vampire girl running across the field towards the church. She then begins to change into a huge bat and flies over towards the churchyard.

Lewis couldn't believe his eyes then remembered his mum and dad downstairs. He jumps up but just as he is about to take his eyes from the window, he notices his mum walking across the field in a trance headed towards the church.

Lewis calls out through the window.

"Mum."

He runs to the door and unlocks it as fast as he can, then down the stairs. He reaches the kitchen door then suddenly the door opens. Carlos is standing, his shirt still open, looking a little messed up.

"Dad, are you OK?"

"I'm fine, where is Mum?"

"She's on the way to the graveyard following that woman."

Carlos looked confused.

"The graveyard?"

"Yes."

"What woman?"

"You don't remember, do you?"

"Remember what, my head is a bit muzzy?"

"Come with me... Hurry."

"Lewis what are you going on about?"

Lewis grabs his dad's coat and gives it to him.

"It's late; it's too late to be playing games like this."

Carlos puts on his coat and then goes to the sink and fills his hands with water and quickly washes his face hoping that will clear his muzzy head.

"I'm not playing games, come on Dad."

Carlos and Lewis leave the house in a hurry and speed off across the field. They hide behind a bush, watching the church, waiting.

Carlos is still light headed and muzzy and really not sure what he is doing.

"You still haven't explained why we are here. What are we looking for?"

"Dad, to be honest I'm not sure."

"Well, let's go back until you are sure. We need to find your mum. I think that is more important right now."

"Shhhhhhh, Dad. That's what we are doing now."

"Well she isn't going to be here. We should go before the police come. They will think we are a couple of perverts."

Carlos is about to get up when Lewis pulls his arm.

"Shhhh... look."

"Where?"

Lewis points to the church corner.

"Over there by the corner."

Three vampires are walking towards the crypt. As far as Carlos can see they are just three women walking in a graveyard at a stupid hour of the night.

"What the hell are they doing out here?"

The vampires walk up to the crypt door and slowly turn into mist and seep under the door one by one. Carlos cannot believe what he is seeing.

Carlos jumps up and puts his hands on his head.

"What the fuck, what the fuck have I just watched here? What the hell?! I don't understand."

"Neither do I, Dad."

"What about your mum?"

"She is probably inside."

Carlos freaks out again.

"What? Inside that crypt? What the hell would she be doing in the crypt? I don't understand what this has got to do with your mum, Lewis?"

"Dad, will you just listen, please? I saw one of them in the kitchen. I think they have Mum now. I think she was bitten."

"What?"

"They are vampires, Dad. One of them was in the house."

Carlos sits down on the damp grass and puts his head in his hands.

"Let me get this straight. What we have just seen are vampires and one of them has bitten your mum and turned her into a vampire and taken her into that crypt?"

Lewis puts his arm over his dad's shoulder.

"Dad, to be honest I don't know where Mum has gone but I did see her walking this way toward the church."

"Then we have to go and see if she is in there."

"No, Dad, No! It's too dangerous we have to get prepared."

Carlos and Lewis get up and start to walk back to the house.

"How do they do that?"

"I don't know they just do."

"Anyway, prepared? What do you mean? How can you prepare for that? It's crazy."

"We have to stick together on this. We have to do this right or they would kill us too."

Carlos puts his arm around Lewis' shoulder and gives him a gentle squeeze.

"This is like some fucking nightmare."

**

As Carlos and Lewis approach their garden, they notice Tanya lying on the lawn, Carlos rushes over to her and Lewis runs after him.

Carlos lifts her up into the sitting position and kisses her.

"Tanya, what happened?"

She is pale and begins to shake as she opens her eyes.

"Where am I?"

"Your home, everything will be OK, you just …"

Lewis jumps in before Carlos says anything he shouldn't. They didn't want to frighten or confuse her.

"Mum, it was just a bad dream."

"A dream, what time is it?"

"Never mind, let's get you inside."

Carlos picks her up and carries her into the house.

As they enter the kitchen, Carlos puts Tanya down. She steadies herself and sits on a chair at the dinner table, still shuddering and looking a little vacant.

"Lewis, can you get Mum's coat and put it over her shoulders?"

Lewis runs into the hall and grabs Tanya's coat from the coat stand then runs back to the kitchen and drapes it over Tanya's shoulders. He gently rubs her shoulders. While doing this, he notices two puncture marks on her neck, he inhales a little but just enough for Tanya to notice. She turns her head and notices Lewis' expression.

"What's the matter darling?"

"Nothing."

Tanya makes an attempt at a smile. Carlos notices the uneasiness of the situation.

"I'll get you a drink. And then bed, OK?"

"Just water."

***

Lewis sat at his desk in his bedroom, the computer switched on, flicking through the internet, reading up on vampires, folklore and legends. He finds an interesting article on vampires – *Fact or Fiction*. After reading the article he clicks print, the printer clicks away and then churns out two sheets of A4 with the very article that Lewis needed. Lewis checks that everything has printed OK. He then leans back in his chair and reads it once again.

Grabbing a pen from his drawer, he picks up a notepad and starts making notes; he marks the header as 'notes' and underlines it twice with his pen before writing number one: holy water.

***

Riding Carlos like a wild animal, she flings back her long blonde hair. Some has stuck to the perspiration on her face, the rest swinging up and down in frantic movements that her body commands; Carlos orgasms.

"Fuck me, no, fuck me."

Carlos carries on thrusting until Tanya screams out loud with final ecstasy.

Tanya slides Carlos's flaccid but meaty penis from inside her and sits on the edge of the bed; Carlos rubs her side.

"You OK, babe?"

She ignores him completely, pausing as if in some sort of trance only for a few seconds, she then gets up off the bed and walks slowly over to the door. She takes her pink fluffy dressing gown, which is hanging on the back of the door, and puts it on.

"I need the bathroom."

Carlos was lying still on his back with his eyes closed, the perspiration still running from his forehead.

"OK babe."

Tanya watches Carlos as she stands in the door way. She watches him turn over onto his side. Quite emotionless, she leaves the bedroom and closes the door. Tanya walks slowly across the landing. The old floorboards, under the thick carpet pile, still creak and moan under her feet as she walks towards the bathroom door.

The bathroom door was old and fairly thin and was on Carlos's list of things to do. Tanya had already expressed her wish to have a whole new bathroom fitted.

Tanya closed the door behind her and locked the door; she stood staring still in a trance like state just for a few seconds before opening the small bathroom window.

The window was oblong and fairly narrow with frosted glass. It was the newest part of the bathroom barley, one year old. Before the bathroom suffered with damp and the window was a main factor contributing to it, so after having the walls treated and the new window put in the damp stopped. Now instead of smelling damp and musty, it smells of coconut and pine.

Tanya turns around and faces the sink, she turns on the tap in the basin and leaves her fingers under the tap until the water became warm. She cups her hands and begins to wet her face. The mirror steams up as the sink filled with hot water, the flannel, drapes over into the sink, slips into the bottom. Tanya pulls out the flannel and squeezes out excess water then places the flannel over her face like a mask, steaming the pores of her skin.

Behind her, mist crept down the wall from the bathroom window.

Tanya drops the flannel in the sink and notices through the steamed up mirror a faint figure. She wipes the mirror and notices a woman hovering in the air behind her.

The woman has long dark hair, dark brown eyes and red lips and pale skin, she is quite beautiful – without warning her face changes. She opens her mouth revealing long canine fangs; she lunges down and sinks her fangs into Tanya's neck.

After a short while of drinking the blood and draining what life Tanya had left in her body, the vampire lets Tanya drop to the floor. She opens her mouth like a vice holding a piece of metal. Tanya fell to the floor with a thud into a helpless bundle. The vampire stares at Tanya's useless body, her blood red eyes wide open as the blood of Tanya ran from her mouth.

Chapter Eight

The morning sun was low and shining through Constable Connors office window.

9:15 am exactly. The phone hadn't stopped with stupid calls about the power cut that had happened due to the storm.

Mrs Stonebridge had lost the contents of her freezer because it had defrosted and no one was answering her calls at Cornwall Electric. She was in complete darkness and was panicking just like the other eighteen people. Most of them were pensioners, in their seventies and eighties. All complaining that no one was answering the phones at Cornwall Electric.

Constable Connor was keeping his patients because that was the kind of man he was plus the fact that it was his job. He was trying to explain, it was because of the storm and it had knocked out the lines in that area and that they were being fixed, but to be patient.

Sometimes Constable Conner's work would be boring and nothing much happening due to the fact that nothing much does happen in that part of Cornwall, sometimes the highlight of his week is sorting out lost property that had been handed in.

This morning another call from Jack Butler's wife and George Turner's wife, both ringing to say they hadn't returned home and were worried.

They couldn't contact them on the phone either because of the phone lines being down and both were concerned in case they had had an accident in the boat in the storm.

Constable Conner's calmed Mrs Turner down when she phoned headquarters.

"Now don't you worry we will head out right away and make sure everything is OK."

"OK Constable, I really do appreciate it. Mrs Turner is worried too, young Freddy's mum is here with me, she's panicking."

"Just try to keep calm; I'm sure it's nothing to worry about."

***

The sea was much calmer; in fact it was rather a pleasant short trip on this old police boat.

Even the sky was blue apart from a few clouds in the distance. The lighthouse looked like a postcard against that rich blue September sky, with the sun hitting it, highlighting every sharp rock and exaggerating the brightness of the white washed tower.

As they pulled up and moored next to the lighthouse boat, Sergeant Pike looked straight at Connor and Constable Connor looked straight at Sergeant Pike simultaneously.

"That's strange?"

Constable Conner agreed with just a slight nod of his head.

They climb up onto the rocks, then on to the small path leading up to the lighthouse entrance. The door was open.

Sergeant Pike suddenly steps back as he notices Rusty lying on the floor. His throat had been ripped out and he was still lying in his own blood. His eyes wide open and tongue hanging limp from his open mouth.

"What the hell happened here?"

"I don't know Sergeant, but I don't like it at all. Let's go up."

They proceed up the staircase to the open door of the radio room.

"Oh my god."

Constable Connor immediately calls for air ambulance on his radio while Sergeant Pike checks out the bodies.

"Constable they are white as sheets."

"It's because they are dead, Pike."

"Yes, I know that but how did they die?"

"I have no idea but this one looks like it's been dropped from a height."

Chapter Nine

Lewis holding the door handle, rattles the bathroom door again then slaps his hands on the side of his legs in agitation. Sighing he moves across the landing at a pace and raps on his mum and dad's bedroom door. There is no answer so he raps again.

"Dad?"

Lewis knocks again.

"Mum, Dad?"

Lewis slowly opens the bedroom door and sees that his dad is lying star fished across the bed sound asleep.

His mum isn't in the room. Lewis's first thoughts were *Mum must be in the bathroom but why doesn't she answer?*

Lewis attempts to wake his dad by shaking him gently.

"Dad, Dad wake up… Dad."

Carlos stirs and rolls over and slowly opens his eyes.

"Hey what's up, what time is it?"

"It's gone 10 am."

"Really? Shit."

"I need the bathroom, it's locked."

Carlos looks at Tanya's pillow and then back at Lewis.

"It'll be your mum."

Carlos holds his head as he sits up in the bed.

"Damn my head, I must have slept heavy."

"Dad it's been locked all night."

Carlos looks confused.

"All night? Are you sure?"

Lewis nods. Carlos immediately jumps up out of the bed just wearing his Calvin Klein white underwear and runs out of the bedroom and runs to the bathroom door. Lewis follows behind.

Carlos bangs on the bathroom door. Lewis can see the panic on his dad's face.

Everything is going through Lewis's mind, maybe she has passed out; maybe she has fallen into a deep sleep, everything but what really has happened behind that door.

Carlos continues to bang on the door and call to Tanya.

"Tanya, are you OK, can you open the door, babe? Please!"

Nothing. Not a word, just silence.

Before Lewis could finish speaking.

"What are we going to do, Dad?"

Carlos bangs the door open with his shoulder; luckily the door was old and flimsy.

The door swung open and banged against the wall and bounced back off of Carlos's shoulder.

It was like déjà vu finding Tanya again lying still on the ground, this time on the bathroom floor.

Her eyes wide open, her skin as white as the bathroom tiles, her mouth open and her lips as white as her cheeks. There are patches of blood all over the floor, mostly soaked up in her pink dressing gown. The puncture wounds on her neck were larger and more swollen and covered in blood.

Carlos cries out knowing the worst.

"No!"

He falls to his knees and holds her, cradling her, fighting back the tears. Lewis is standing in shock; he didn't say a word he just stood staring at his mum. The tears just running down his face, he gulps back the saliva that had run down into his throat, then notices the bathroom window wide open.

After a few moments, his dad stands up and holds Lewis close to him.

"Oh man, she's gone boy, she's gone."

"Dad look, the window."

Carlos looks at the open window then at Tanya then at Lewis.

"Is that how?"

"Yes, Dad they must have come in through the window."

***

Carlos is sitting in Tanya's favourite armchair, the one that's closest to the open log fire which is still waiting to be reignited; the cosy living room sure could do with warming up as Carlos is close to shivering, still in shock from the morning events.

Lewis brings in on a tray; two teas and some biscuits.

Lewis is a good lad, barely thirteen but quite grown up for his age, being an only child, he has always been a little spoilt. Tanya always let him get away with murder whereas Carlos was always the one to put his foot down and said no when he thought it was appropriate.

Today Carlos is lost, he only has Lewis and Lewis seems to understand more about what is going on than Carlos does for a change; it's like role reversal at the moment.

"They should be here soon."

Lewis puts the tray down onto the vanished wooden top coffee table.

"The ambulance?"

"Yeah."

Carlos picks up his tea and sips it.

"Ah, that's good. Do you know I never realised until now you make tea exactly like your mum?"

"Really?"

"Yeah you do, funny I've never noticed that before."

Lewis smiles quite pleased with himself that his dad was feeling happy at least about something today.

The sound of the ambulance is loud; it stops as it pulls up outside the house.

Three ambulance men get out just as Sergeant Pike and Constable Connor pull up in the police car.

***

Mrs Brown is tapping in the price of the groceries on her old-fashioned silver-grey till from the 1990s. She still prefers the old ways and refuses to move with the times and is never shy in telling people that her old till is more reliable.

Mrs Brown is a short tubby and round-faced lady in her sixties; her cheeks are as rosy and shiny as a freshly picked apple. She always keeps a hanky tucked up her sleeve and is never seen without her white freshly ironed apron with a pocket on the front which she keeps all sorts of handy items in such as pens scissors and tape.

Mrs Brown always manages to hear all the gossip in the village first. How she manages this is a mystery to everyone but all the locals say to each other, "We'll ask Mrs Brown, I'm sure she will know."

It's really quite a stand in joke among the local villagers.

As the till adds up, Mrs Brown packs Sally's bag.

"They found her lying there on the floor."

"That poor boy. What was it that she died of, do you know?"

"I don't know, but finding your mother like that. Carlos and Lewis must be devastated."

Sally puts her hand over her mouth and shakes her head thinking about Carlos and Lewis.

"I will have to go and pay my respects; I will go and see them later today. See if they need any help with funeral arrangements and stuff."

Mrs Brown pauses for a second thinking about Susan Moorcroft, the poor girl from the post office.

"I doubt it will be more than a couple of days. They don't seem to hang about here; I suppose that's the beauty of living in a small village."

Sally nods her head in agreement.

"Susan Moorcroft's funeral is tomorrow you know at 11 am. They didn't waste any time with that one, did they? She's barely cold, I shouldn't wonder."

"I know I'm going to it. But Tanya, she was so fit and healthy. She went to the gym twice a week, I can't believe it."

"There is something strange going on. All these young girls just dying like that. They are dropping like flies."

Mrs Brown stops for a second watching Sally's reaction almost revelling in the juicy gossip.

"It's not just the girls. What about those men at the light house?"

"Yes. That poor boy Freddy, he was only in his 40s, no age at all."

Mrs Brown carefully lowers a carton of eggs into Sally's bag. Sally adds to the story.

"Even George's dog, Rusty, apparently had his throat ripped out."

"Oh no."

Mrs Brown gets her hanky out and wipes her nose, then lifts her glasses up and wipes a tear from her left eye.

"I didn't know that. The poor little thing! Who could do a thing like that?"

"I know, that's exactly what I thought"

"That's 27.95 p, my dear."

Sally opens up her small handbag that she has draped over her shoulder and finds her tiny purse, opens it up and produces a visa card and hands it to Mrs Brown.

"I don't know. But the poor police are running around in circles."

Mrs Brown inserts the card into the machine, Sally keys in her number, the receipt rolls out from the back and Mrs Brown rips it off and hands it to Sally. Mrs Brown nods her head in agreement.

"I bet they are. I bet they've never been this busy before. It's usually so quiet around here. See you tomorrow."

Sally lifts her shopping bag from the counter and walks over to the door.

"No doubt, it's still a bit of a worry though. See you soon."

Mrs Brown calls out just as she's closing the door.

"Don't forget to let me know how you get on at Carlos'."

Sally waves through the shop window, Mrs Brown waves back.

Chapter Ten

The moon was almost full tonight shining in the clear night sky. You could almost count every star in the sky it was so clear. So different from the weather they had had over the past couple of days.

There was a chill in the air tonight, feeling a little cooler than it had been. It is nights like this when you can almost feel the winter fast approaching.

Edith Brooks is walking back with her six-year-old granddaughter Pipa, who is skipping in front, all in a world of her own, still wearing her party hat.

Edith loves to watch her as she plays her childish games. Edith is a slender lady of seventy-eight and is fairly agile for her age, she wears her salt and pepper hair up, whiter than pepper probably but nevertheless always immaculate, as is her dress, with little court shoes on her size five feet.

They are on the way back from Pipa's best friend Alice's seventh birthday party, so Pipa is still full of life. She is still buzzing with excitement from the birthday party.

"Grandma, watch."

Pipa does a cartwheel on the cold stone slabbed pavement.

"Isn't it a lovely evening, Pipa?"

Pipa looks at Edith and smiles.

"It's so peaceful after all that noise at the party. Not even a bird singing. But we did have a lovely time didn't we, with all your friends."

Pipa stops skipping in her tracks.

"And the magician."

Pipa waits for Edith to catch up then she hold her hand.

"Yes, and the magician."

Pipa looks up at Edith with her big blue eyes.

"Grandma, can we have some cake when we get home?"

"Yes, of course. I have your cake in my bag and your lolly."

Pipa's eyes light up. She tilts her head on to the side and puts her tiny index finger to her small pink lips.

"Grandma?"

"Yes?"

"Grandma, can I have my lolly now please?"

Edith smiles and strokes the side of Pipa's face.

"Well, since you have been such a good girl and since you asked so nicely, you may."

They both stop walking while Edith unzips the top of her hand bag and moves a few things around inside before she takes out Pipa's lolly. Pipa holds out her tiny hand.

"Hang on a moment, let me take the wrapper off for you."

Edith carefully takes off the wrapper and hands Pipa the strawberry flavoured lolly.

"Thank you, Grandma!"

Pipa wastes no time in sucking and slurping on the lolly. Edith takes hold of Pipa's hand as they cross the road towards the church. The bins outside the church looking almost ready to be emptied, shaded by large yew trees.

As they pass the bins, Edith drops the rubbish into a gap. Pipa looks through the gate at the entrance of the church yard.

"Grandma, is that where Grandad is sleeping with Jesus?"

"Yes darling, sort of."

Just outside the gate and fenced off area outside the church, there is a grass verge, slightly overgrown with dandelions and various weeds and where nettles are growing. Pipa bends down and picks a few of the dandelions.

"Grandma, can I give these flowers to Grandad?"

"OK darling, but we mustn't be too long, it's going to be dark soon."

Edith opens the churchyard gate; it is still in need of some oil judging by the squeak. Edith closes the gate behind them and as soon as they enter a breeze seems to pick up, as if it knew they were there.

The church looks shaded in places towering above the tombs. The evening draws in and the clock face on the church has begun to glow showing the time clearly.

The time is 7:10 pm. Edith checks her wrist watch against the church clock, as most people do as they pass the church, even the vicar does and Edith has seen him do this before church on Sunday while waiting for his flock to arrive.

The path is winding through the churchyard darting in and out around the graves; Pipa is checking every gravestone trying to read them. Edith watches, feeling very pleased to see her taking an interest in history as she carefully tries to read out the dates.

Pipa stops and runs back to Edith and holds her hand again.

"Will you go to sleep with Grandad here, Grandma?"

Taken aback, Edith laughs.

"Well, yes, but not for a long time yet, I hope."

"Good, because I don't want you to leave me ever, Grandma."

Edith feels quite emotional inside and bends down and gives Pipa a kiss and a hug.

"Don't you worry darling, I'm not going anywhere. Come on, let's find your grandad."

After wandering further into the rather vast graveyard, they eventually find Fredrick Brook's headstone, Pipa's grandad and Edith's beloved husband of 47 years, until that damn prostate cancer took his life three years ago.

There is a small vase of dying flowers just in front of the marble headstone. Edith removed the dead flowers and Pipa replaces the flowers with her handful of dandelions.

"There you go, Grandad."

Edith kneels down and pulls out the weeds around the grave.

Pipa wanders off, checking out the headstones, she disappears around the corner and out of Edith's sight.

Edith was preoccupied tidying up Fredrick's grave and hadn't noticed.

Pipa notices a fresh grave and close by some more dandelions. She rushes over and picks them, as she gets up she realises that the new grave only has dead flowers laying on the soil, so she kneels down on the grave and makes a hole. She plants the dandelions and stands up on the grave and stares down, proud of her freshly picked flowers and smiles.

The ground begins to tremble and without warning she is suddenly pulled down into the soil, deep into the grave, only leaving her party hat to roll off in the breeze.

Edith gets up and brushes her hands together.

"There, now isn't that much better?"

Edith realises Pipa isn't there and looks around standing on the spot at first.

"Pipa?"

There is no answer.

"Pipa, Pipa, where are you darling?"

Edith wanders around calling out; she looks up at the sky and realises that it is getting darker and blacker as night draws in. This time of the year it can be dark by 8 pm.

Edith feels a little sick as she starts to panic.

"Pipa, Pipa, answer me, where are you? Come on, we have to get home, Pipa. I have your cake."

As Edith walks around a large yew tree, she sees a woman holding Pipa's hand.

The girl was dressed all in white and looking very pale and gaunt with brown hair down to her neck, her eyes large and dark. Edith didn't notice how strange the girl was, she was just relieved to see Pipa.

"Ah, Pipa, darling, you had me worried."

Edith bends down and gives Pipa a big hug.

"Now don't you go running off like that again."

Edith looks up at the woman.

"Thank you for looking after her."

The woman stares at Edith, her eyes are piercing and Edith gets a chill down her spine. The woman's eyes open wide and the whites of her eyes turn to blood red. She suddenly grabs hold of Edith by the throat and yanks her neck back with such force her neck cracks. She sinks her long fangs into Edith's neck; the blood shoots from the corners of the vampire's mouth, as the jugular pulsates out the warm blood from Edith's throat. As she drinks the blood, the vampire doesn't take her eyes off of Pipa, their eyes locked into each other's. Edith drops to the floor in a heap after the vampire finishes feeding. Pipa smiles, she takes hold of the woman's hand and walks towards the crypt door.

The vampire stops then picks up Pipa with both arms and savagely bites her on the neck. After only a short time, she throws Pipa across the cemetery like a rag doll. Walking towards the crypt, she wipes the blood from her mouth with the back of her hand.

As she approaches the crypt door she transforms into mist, which seeps under the door and into the crypt.

Chapter Eleven

Two white tents have been erected over the two bodies of Pipa and Edith. Forensic officers are in and out of the tents, the whole area has been cordoned off with police tape, with a few police keeping the public at bay.

Sergeant Pike is chatting to Larry about the incident and Larry is quite nervous and looking quite upset.

There is a small crowd of people attending the funeral of Susan Moorcroft in the distance; they are oblivious to the comings and goings around the tents and the investigation of two more murders.

"What about the gates? Do you ever lock them?"

"No sergeant, the gates are never locked, we never have. You see there is a path that cuts right through. I suppose people use it as a short cut, so we keep the gates unlocked."

A young looking police officer approaches Sergeant Pike and cuts in on the conversation.

"Excuse me sergeant. Can I have a word?"

Sergeant Pike puts his hand on the officer's shoulder as they walk away from Larry.

"Excuse me a moment, Larry."

"The forensics believe that they both suffered the same fatality. Apart from the little girl, who's back and legs where broken."

Sergeant Pike exhales for a moment then looks at his watch. It is 12:10 pm.

"Did they say how?"

"No, they said an injury like that could have only been caused by a fall from a great height, apparently the bones broke on impact."

"What the hell are we dealing with here?"

***

As the coffin lowers into the grave the crowd stare in silence dressed in their best black attire.

Susan would have probably had everyone dressed in bright colours because that was the type of person she was, nothing ever really matched with Susan, as she had no colour coordination at all. Odd socks sometimes, odd trainers just an odd young woman, in the nicest of senses. Putting all that aside she really was a lovely and popular girl at the post office.

There were only a few people crying, the rest were just in shock. It's so hard to accept or to believe such a young girl of twenty four could be taken so soon.

The vicar of St John's Church glances up at the crowd watching the coffin descend into the dark hole torn and cut with great precision, from the different colours of the earth.

A pile of soil lies just to the side, awaiting the shovel to fill up the hole and cover the pine wood coffin.

"Because God has chosen to call our sister from this life to himself, we commit her body to the earth, for we are dust and unto dust we shall return."

Larry picks up the big bag of weeds and leaves that he had tied up in an experienced knot on the top; he had mastered this no matter how full a bag was.

Larry wanders up the path carrying his bag of rubbish in one hand swinging his keys in the other, he heads towards the gate, he glances over his shoulder as the crowd start to leave one by one.

***

Peter watches the last of the crowd leave the funeral then takes one last look into the grave and crosses himself.

"May you rest in peace."

Peter is a very popular and much loved vicar in this small village and has been with St John's church for almost twenty years. He seems to remember everyone's names – even the non-church-goers.

He is a kind, friendly, and softly spoken man in his fifties.

About six feet tall with greying hair brushed back into a widow's peak with blue eyes and just a few little laughter lines. His face is fair with slightly gaunt features showing off his high cheekbones.

Chapter Twelve

St John's Church sits still and cool against the moonlit sky. The stain glass windows shimmer and glow as they catch the light of the moon; otherwise the colour of the glass remains dark as the lead frames that hold them.

Tonight the wind is up, you can hear it howling and singing through the yew trees of the churchyard.

There is silence, not a bird not even an owl, just complete silence, there is an eerie emptiness a strange feeling in the night air.

There is a sudden bang that echoes across the graveyard as dirt flies high into the air, raining down on the surrounding graves and tombs.

A coffin lid falls down and embeds itself deep into the soil, close to the grave like a shovel hitting the sand with force.

As mist clears from the open grave, Susan Moorcroft is lying in her coffin sleeping the sleep of the undead.

Her eyes open, they are blood red.

Her legs do not even bend as she rises from her coffin; she just elevates vertically, then rises up to ground level.

Slowly she walks past the coffin lid sticking out from the soil like an open door.

She stops and looks up towards the moon and as she does the moonlight catch her red eyes, her pale skin and her white sharp fangs.

Susan walks slowly towards the crypt door across the graveyard. As she reaches the door, she turns to mist that seeps under the door.

***

The sky is pale blue, only a few scattered clouds. Although the wind is cool, it is going to be a pleasant day. Well, that is what Larry thought as he opens the gate and walks up the path in the graveyard.

In the distance, Larry could see the coffin lid sticking out of the ground, it really wasn't that clear until he got closer and realised it really was a coffin lid, just perched there, erect and bold as brass embedded deep in the soil.

"Well, I'll be buggered, what the hell is going on here?"

Larry then spots the open grave of Susan Moorcroft, he stands and thinks for a minute. *Who on earth would want to steal a body and who would want to vandalise, desecrate and completely destroy a grave,* he thought, all these things bouncing to and fro inside his head.

In the distance, he notices Peter walking towards him.

Larry runs ahead and meets him before he sees what has happened to Susan's grave.

"Good morning, Larry."

"Do you have a minute, Peter?"

"Of course I do, what's the problem?"

Larry just slightly out of breath and confused as he tries to explain the best he can.

"Well I don't know if it's a problem. More of a crime I'd say. This is the second grave I have found empty in a week."

Peter shakes his head also looking quite baffled.

"I don't understand? What grave?"

"Neither do I. It's Susan's. We bury them and the next day they're gone."

"Gone? What do you mean gone?"

"Just as I said, we bury them one day and… Look, come with me."

Larry and Peter rush over to Susan's grave, as soon as Peter sees the empty coffin he crosses himself.

"Good God, we need to inform the police at once."

"OK, I will make a call," he takes out a rather dirty and old looking mobile phone and begins to dial.

"I told them about the last one."

"It's happened before?"

"Oh yes, only a few days ago."

Larry stops dialling and looks up at Peter realising he has some explaining to do.

"You should have told me about this."

"To be honest Peter, I didn't want to alarm you."

"Well, you should have, its sacrilege. What did the police have to say about it?"

Peter takes another look into the grave.

"They said they would look into it."

"Larry, you really should have told me. Oh, well I suppose we will just have to wait and see."

"Shall I call them now?"

"Yes, yes we need them here."

Larry dials again on his dirty old phone.

"You were away on the day the body went missing. But you're right, I should have told you. I'm sorry, Peter. Oh hello, is that Constable Connor?"

"No, it's Sergeant Pike. Is that Larry?"

"Yes, it is."

"What can I do for you?"

"Well, sergeant, well it's happened again. Another body has gone missing."

"What the hell is happening?"

"Can you come?"

"Sure, we will as quick as we can."

Larry hangs up and puts the phone back in his pocket.

"They will be down as quick as possible."

Peter begins to walk away.

"They know where I am if they need to talk with me."

"I suppose it's hard to do a missing person profile when they've just been buried…"

Peter stops walking, then decides not to react to Larry's comment, he continues to walk away towards his office at the back of the church.

***

Peter had a full on day today what with four funerals; Freddy, Jack, George and his dog Rusty. It was going to be quite busy.

The crowd was small and stayed practically the whole day as they knew all the men that worked on the lighthouse, even Rusty, the dog.

As the crowd eventually disappeared from the funerals, the vicar made his way back to the church for some quite time and prayer.

The graves, all in a row, lay cold and still as the evening sky turned black.

Chapter Thirteen

Carlos is sitting in his dressing gown at the kitchen table; the pink clock on the wall is ticking softly as the clock moves to 12:35 pm.

The kettle clicks off as the steam pours from the spout.

Carlos gets up slowly, in a daze still partly from a deep sleep and partly because he has so much going through his head. Today he really is not feeling himself.

He pours the hot water into his coffee mug and then realises he has got Tanya's cup out, he stares at her cup before he puts it back in the cupboard.

As he pours the milk into the mug, he glances out across the field. Today it looks like rain; it's still looking fairly dark, such a contrast to yesterday's blue sky and sun.

As he sits back down at the kitchen table, he snatches a photo of Tanya laughing from the notice board. It was one that Lewis took of his mum while on holiday at some beach resort along the coast.

Sitting down at the kitchen table, holding the photograph in both hands, nipping the edges between his fingers so as not to cover any of the pictures. Carlos begins to remember.

Flashbacks; terrible flashbacks. They are as clear and as horrible as they were on the actual evening just a few nights ago.

All he can see is Tanya lying on the kitchen floor in a heap, her eyes shut tight as blood runs down the side of her head and down her face.

The sweat is building up on Carlos' forehead as the images flash in his mind. The kitchen door opens and in walks Lewis. He walks straight to the kettle, only glancing over at his dad.

"Hey Dad, you want a coffee?"

Carlos barely hears him.

"Err, what, oh no thanks, I just got me one."

Lewis grabs the coffee from the cupboard and puts half a spoon of instant in the mug. Lewis doesn't like his coffee too strong, not like Carlos who loves the kick of a strong coffee. He then adds two spoons of sugar.

"Dad?"

Carlos is just staring at the photograph of Tanya.

"Dad, are you OK?"

Carlos just stares into nothing. This time in his flashback, it is clearer than ever. He sees the woman in the kitchen, her eyes blood red as she looks at him. She then tips her head back opening her mouth wide, showing her sharp white fangs.

The sudden realisation hits him as he shouts out, "Vampires? Shit, no fucking way!"

Lewis brings his coffee over and sits at the table opposite his dad.

"I know it's hard to believe but it's the only explanation."

"But its old horror book stuff. Movies and shit."

Carlos wipes the sweat from his head with the sleeve of his dressing gown.

"It's true Dad, you have seen for yourself."

"But who the hell is going to believe us. I mean we're not dealing with humans here. These are… who can we tell? How can you kill these things?"

Lewis looks straight into his dad's eyes.

"A wooden stake through the heart?"

"Come on, Lewis, this is not Ingrid Pitt we're dealing with here. This is the real thing. It might not work. Then what?"

Lewis looks a little deflated and stuck for words or answers.

"Yes, you're right Dad, but at least we know where they sleep."

Carlos bangs his head in his hands in frustration.

"This is a fucking dream. I'm gonna wake up in a minute. Tell me all of this is a fucking dream."

"A nightmare Dad. It's a nightmare and I'm so frightened."

Lewis begins to show tears in his eyes, Carlos looks up after hearing a tremble in Lewis's voice. He sees a tear roll down Lewis's face. Carlos reaches out and grabs Lewis's hands.

"Hey, come here boy."

Lewis gets up and puts his arms around his dad's neck.

Carlos hugs Lewis tight as he looks over his shoulder, out across the field.

***

Larry wheels his barrow full of weeds and old flowers past the crypt door, one of the flowers falls from the barrow as it hits a bump; it lands at the foot of the crypt door.

As Larry turns the corner and heads towards the small pile of dead leaves and rubbish ready for burning the flower shrivels up and dies. Once starting out as a beautiful red rose with only a couple of withered dead leaves, now a rotten brown weed.

Chapter Fourteen

Carlos parks up almost outside the church. They both jump out. Lewis slams his door shut and Carlos locks up his jeep with his remote on his key ring.

They open the churchyard gate and walk up the winding path to the church.

"I didn't used to mind cutting through here. Now I hate it."

"I know, son."

The door is open to the church, Peter is sitting on a pew at the front of the church with his eyes closed, probably praying or thinking about what has been happening recently in his church and around the village.

Carlos quietly walks up to Peter, so as not to disturb him. They sit down in the pew behind him.

Carlos whispers to Peter, "Peter?"

Peter jumps and gives a little yelp which resounds around the church; the acoustics are something special at St John's church.

"Oh, you gave me a start."

"Oh, sorry vicar, you're a little jumpy."

Peter shakes Carlos's hand.

"Ah, its Carlos, isn't it?"

He smiles when he sees Lewis.

"And you must be Lewis."

"Yes, I am."

Lewis holds his hand out waiting for the vicar to shake it. When the Vicar obliges, Lewis gives him a big grin. The Vicar stands up and Carlos and Lewis both follow and stand up too.

"I'm sorry about Tanya. It is very sad. How are you both coping?"

"Not brilliantly, to be honest."

"That is to be expected."

"Vicar..."

The Vicar cuts in and puts his hand on Carlos's shoulder stopping him from speaking, the Vicar pauses and looks at Carlos straight in the eye and smiles.

"Call me Peter; it's much better than vicar, isn't it?"

"Peter, I have something... a matter to discuss with you and it's not an easy one."

Peter walks ahead down the isle of the church, Carlos follows followed by Lewis.

"Funeral stuff I expect, now don't worry everything has been taken care of by..."

Carlos catches up and holds Peters arm and with all seriousness he tries to deliver his statement without sounding ridiculous.

"No, no, I wish it was that simple. I'm going to tell you something now, and I don't want you thinking I'm going mad or anything. What I am going to tell you is completely true."

Lewis looks up at the Peter and nods profusely.

"It's about how Tanya died. She was killed, murdered!"

Peter looked quite shocked.

"I'm so sorry. I never knew that."

"No, it's not that simple. Oh god, I'm sorry, listen, Peter do you believe in the occult, in ghost's supernatural, life after death?"

"What like heaven, meeting our maker? Is that what you mean?"

"No. Not that sort of life after death."

Lewis jumps in with his comment, his very sure statement and as loud as he could.

"The un-dead, vampires?"

Peter stands for a moment just to take in the last conversation and especially Lewis's statement about vampires. Peter begins to chuckle.

"Of course not, that's just fantasy…"

Carlos cuts in before Peter can say anything else.

"Tanya was killed by a vampire."

Peter realises that Carlos is very serious and by the look on Lewis's face he was too.

"Is this some sort of joke?"

Carlos raises his voice but tries to keep a lid on his emotions in front of Lewis.

"Why would I joke about my wife's death? We both saw it. We have both seen them. They are using your crypt to sleep in."

"Them?"

Lewis voices another statement.

"The vampires."

Peter breaks away for a second.

"I'm sorry Carlos, I can't believe this. You can't honestly expect me to believe I have vampires under my church in my crypt. Even if I did believe, and anyone found out I would be struck off… no, I'm sorry."

"Please believe us. Open the crypt let us go in and have a look. It will prove everything. I'm not mad. It's true, we did see it."

Peter looks at Carlos's eyes, he looks like he could cry; he looked frightened, even terrified. A bag of mixed emotions and Lewis looked the same. Lewis pleads with the vicar to believe them.

"Dad is telling the truth. We watched them together, honestly, I promise."

Peter bites his bottom lip as he closes his eyes to think.

"Well, that crypt has been opened only once in the whole time I have served here, and I have been here for thirty six years. I would imagine the lock is rusted now. I'm sorry Carlos. Look, go and get some rest and I will see you tomorrow at the funeral."

Peter watches Carlos and Lewis walking along the church path. He shakes his head and heads on off to the vicarage just behind the church.

Carlos has his arm over Lewis's shoulders.

"I feel like a right idiot."

"Me too. But it's the truth, Dad."

"Yes, I know but who is going to believe us? Now the vicar probably thinks… Oh, God knows what he's thinking now. Come on, get in, let's get home and let's hope curiosity kills the cat."

Lewis looks up completely baffled.

"What?"

"Never mind, just an old saying."

Carlos unlocks the jeep and they both get in, Lewis sits quiet. Carlos notices and puts his hand on his knee and slaps it gently.

"Hey, you OK?"

"Yeah."

"Busy day tomorrow what with Mum's …"

Lewis stops his dad from elaborating.

"Yes, I know Dad."

***

Sally shouts up the stairs.

"Night night, Alison!"

A little voice shouts back down.

"Night Mum!"

Sally smiles and closes the door to the living room and walks over to the window and looks out. Just a few street lamps light up the road, it is so quiet. The windows are starting to get condensation on then as the nights are getting cooler, in fact, quite chilly.

Sally closes her chocolate brown curtains blocking out the cold night. She looks around and there are teddies and dolls lying everywhere, toys in one corner, dolls house in another, it looks just like a toy store that's been ransacked.

Sally just sighs and moves a few teddies from the sofa where Sally had been sitting. She plonks herself down and relaxes with her love story, a novel she had picked up at one of the church fairs recently.

Chapter Fifteen

Well, Carlos was right; curiosity did get the better of Peter. He had got almost to his front door when he decided to turn back and investigate.

He couldn't stop thinking about what Carlos and Lewis had said. It was going round and round inside his head, churning the most fantastical thoughts he had ever imagined or even thought possible.

But what if there was any truth in it? They both really looked like they believed they had seen it or at least seen something they didn't understand.

But the one thing Peter just couldn't get out of his head was the fact that Carlos had said his wife had been murdered. How could he say such a thing if it wasn't true or at least he believed it was true?

Peter had to know what was behind the door of the crypt, just to put his mind at rest and he could then tell Carlos your mind is playing tricks and to get rest or get some help. But why did Lewis say the same?

Peter stood staring at the crypt door, looking all around the frame expecting something to happen, he then puts his ear to the door listening. He couldn't hear anything so he turned and began to walk away but then stopped and began to think again.

He walked back to the door and got out a bunch of keys. He fumbled with the bunch until he found a large silver key and slipped it into the lock, surprisingly it unlocked quite easily.

Peter pushed the door open; the hinges definitely need oil as it squeaked loudly down the crypt stairs.

The stairway was dark and the crypt smelt damp and musty. Peter's eyes were only just adjusting to the dark when he saw the small window, letting in a very small amount of light from the moon and the night sky.

Peter had a small torch attached to his key ring which he always kept to find keyholes when locking the church on those dark evenings. He turned on the torch which was quite powerful and shone the beam of light down the stairs. Cobwebs and spiders ran freely across their thick dusty webs as dust danced in the beam of light.

As he reached the bottom of the stairs a mouse or a rat ran across the floor. It startled him and he stumbled, he steadied himself by holding onto a pillar.

As Peter shone his torch around the crypt, he noticed something very strange; a large oval object lying on the floor. He then noticed another and another.

There were several of these slimy looking things just lying there.

Peter wanted to look closer so he slowly and quietly walked towards one, the one closest to the stairs.

As he approached the slimy object, he shone his torch straight on to it, laminating it like a giant light bulb, a transparent cocoon.

It was almost transparent but what he saw would be an image that would never leave his mind until the day that he died. Inside was a naked body of a woman. Peter quickly shone his torch at another; it was of a naked man and another, a woman. The body inside moved.

Peter shone his torch across to a row of tombs and on them were lying bodies of three women, there was clearly blood around their mouths. Also lying on the floor were bodies of young women, their stomachs looking like they were going to burst.

Peter had never seen anything like this before. He couldn't believe what he was seeing; it was like some sort of a nightmare.

He shines the torch on one of the girl's faces lying on the floor. It was Susan Moorcroft, her eyes open, they were blood red. She opens her mouth and her canine teeth are sharp. Peter gasps and stumbles back.

"Good God, no."

Peter runs as fast as he can, up the crypt stairs and out of the door, he pulls the heavy door shut, panting, as he can he fumbles for his keys. He drops them and quickly he bends down to pick them up.

Peter feels a hand on his shoulder, he jumps letting out a yell.

"In God's name."

Larry is standing there with a torch.

"Did I make you jump? You're working late? What were you doing down there?"

Peter finishes locking the door.

"Err… nothing I… I…"

Larry cuts in noticing the sweat on Peter's forehead shining in the lamplight.

"Looks like you've seen a ghost. Are you OK?"

"Yes, I'm fine. I was just checking these old keys, and you gave me a start."

"OK, see you tomorrow, goodnight sleep well vicar!"

Larry chuckles to himself as he walks off.

***

Lewis's bedside lamp gives out just enough light to read. The quilt pulled up to his chin and his knees bent up so he can rest his book comfortably. A glass of milk sits on his bedside table next to three chocolate biscuits that are resting on a piece of kitchen roll, mainly to soak up the drips that had run down the glass.

Lewis takes after his mum; Tanya loved to read she always had a book by the bed and several under the coffee table in the lounge.

Just as Lewis was getting into his book there was a bang on the bedroom door.

"Yes?"

"Can I come in? Are you decent?"

Before Lewis could answer, Carlos opens the door and walks in.

"You didn't even give me a chance to answer."

"Answer what?"

"Dad? Are you decent, you asked me are you decent and then you just walked straight in?"

Carlos puts his hands in his pockets and sighs as he shrugs his shoulders.

"I'm sorry, my head's a bit messed at the moment, I forgot."

"Don't worry."

Carlos leans over the bed and checks out the front cover of Lewis's book.

"Vampires, really?"

"Yes Dad, vampires. It's about the history and legends, past to present. It's really interesting."

"Frightening, OK. Don't read too late we have to be up early in the morning. Don't forget, church at 10:00 am."

"I know Dad, I'll just finish this chapter then I'll turn out the light."

Carlos feels around his neck for his gold chain and crucifix.

"Don't forget to keep your crucifix on."

"Dad, I don't think they are going to work. I mean, they are living beneath a church."

"Just keep it on in case."

"OK."

Carlos leaves the room and just before the door shuts, he opens it up again.

"Oh, here."

Carlos throws a bulb of garlic onto the bed; Lewis picks it up and smirks.

"Dad! Garlic! Really?"

"Just in case. Night, night."

"Night, Dad."

Carlos closes the door, Lewis shakes his head and smiles. He continues reading while holding onto his crucifix.

Chapter Sixteen

On this cool September morning and the first day of autumn, the sun was hazy in the pale blue sky. It was the first morning Carlos had seen his breath cutting through the morning air.

There was a good turn out to Tanya's funeral as she was a popular young woman in the village; often seen jogging with her fitness tracker on her arm and her earplugs in listening to Randy Travis.

Carlos had converted her somewhat to country music although she still loved her soul music, and quite often she used to have Lionel Richie blaring out from her stereo in the kitchen, as she baked fruit cakes and prepared some surprise for Carlos and Lewis for when they got home.

Mrs Brown had shut her convenience store for a few hours. Sally had also put her home help on hold and even a few of Carlos's work colleagues had come to pay their respects.

Sally was holding Lewis's hand as she held back the tears. Lewis's eyes are red and puffy from crying. His cheeks are wet from the tears. He buries his head in Sally's arms as the coffin lowers into the ground.

Carlos lowers his head, his shoulders shaking as he cries.

Mrs Brown puts her arm around his waist, she also has tears in her eyes. She lifts her glasses to wipe her eyes with a tissue that she had carefully tucked up her sleeve.

After the funeral service is finished, Carlos looked completely lost, his eyes empty, wandering back and forth, thinking and remembering, seeing Tanya's face flashing in his head just telling him not to worry, you will be fine, laughing and smiling. Crazy thoughts flashing in and out of his head.

Carlos walks slowly over to Peter who is thanking the guests for coming. As he does he gets pats on the back and rubs on the shoulders wishing him well.

Mrs Brown rubs Carlos's hand between her hands in an attempt to warm it up. She looks up into his eyes.

"Are you going to be alright, my lovely? If you need anything please just call me, don't hesitate, OK?"

Carlos looks down at Mrs Brown and smiles.

"Sure."

Carlos wipes his eyes with his hanky and puts it back in his pocket; he clears his throat and walks over to Peter.

"Thank you, vicar!"

Peter looks at him and raises his eyebrows and Carlos remembers not to be so formal – it's Peter not vicar anymore.

"Sorry, Peter, it was a good service, you did a great job, thank you."

Peter looks over to Lewis and Carlos looks back over to Lewis, standing looking down at the coffin in the grave.

"Lewis has taken it bad; he was very close to his mum."

Peter nods his head then puts his hand on Carlos's shoulder and looks around to make sure nobody is in earshot.

"May I have a word with you later?"

"Sure."

"Say in about one hour, if that's convenient?"

Carlos looks baffled and Peter notices.

"It is important, Carlos."

"Can I ask what it is about?"

Peter checks once again to make sure nobody is listening.

Then a few more start walking towards Carlos and Peter.

"Carlos, we can talk better in my office at the back of the church. It's important, let's say about 1:30 pm."

"Yes, OK that gives me some time to do a few things."

"See you then."

Sally taps Carlos on the shoulder.

"I'm going now, I have to pick Alison up. If you need anything, please call me. Anything. I don't care what time it is. OK?"

Carlos smiles.

"Thank you, Sally. I will. Thank you for coming."

Only a few more people are left making their way down the path and out of the churchyard. Lewis is still standing at the grave staring down at Tanya's coffin.

Carlos calls Lewis over.

"Lewis, come on boy."

Lewis just looks up and then back down to the coffin.

"I will see you later?"

"Yes, OK."

Carlos walks over to Lewis and stands next to him. He puts his hand around Lewis's shoulders.

"Hey, let's go home."

Carlos gently kisses the top of Lewis's head.

Chapter Seventeen

Just a usual quiet day in Constable Connors office; a small pile of notes and letters to send and some that have been sent, a closed black diary with the police crest stamped on it, a pen that looks like it's just about to roll onto the floor and a corner of the desk where the constable rests his feet when he has forty winks on his tea break after the 'do not disturb' is turned on his door.

The station is run very well and also in a much laidback and quite old-fashioned way, it works for Constable Connor and it works for everyone else, it's hardly Scotland Yard headquarters in this sleepy village of Cornwall.

Constable Connor sits down at his desk and places a freshly made hot steaming cup of coffee strong with one sugar just as he likes it. He sits back in his leather office chair and swings it around and sure enough up go his feet onto the corner of the desk.

Grabbing the report left on his desk with one hand and his coffee in the other Constable Connor begins to read the report stamped 'urgent'.

After a few moments of reading, Constable Connors facial expression changes from one of boredom to one of shock.

"Good God."

He swings his feet around onto the floor and takes a quick slurp of his coffee and rushes to his office door which he opens so fast it bangs into the filing cabinet.

He spots Sergeant Pike wrestling with a pile of folders.

"Pike, are you busy?"

Sergeant Pike places the folders down carefully on the large table in the middle of the room; they slide all over the place.

"Shit."

Sergeant Pike attempts to tidy them up.

"Leave them for a moment, come with me."

Sergeant Pike follows Constable Connor into his office.

"Close the door."

Constable Connor sits down and gestures to Pike.

"Sit down."

He hands him the report.

"Have a read of this, it's from the pathology department."

Sergeant Pike begins to read the document as Constable Connor watches Sergeant Pikes face change.

"Well what do you make of that?"

"I don't know sir, unbelievable. All of them the same."

Constable Connor sips his coffee then nods.

"Yes, the same; all of them. All with less than half their blood left. Almost completely drained."

Sergeant Pike pauses for a second as he thinks.

"Constable?"

The constable raises his eyebrows as Sergeant Pike continues.

"But there was no blood at any of the crime scenes. None!"

"Yes I know. I'm completely baffled."

Sergeant Pike jokes but in a sort of serious way.

"Vampires!"

Constable Connor takes his remark literally.

"But it's impossible surely."

Sergeant crosses his arms and stares at Constable Connor.

"Ah, this is Cornwall 2021 not Transylvania 1821."

Sergeant Pike chuckles at Constable Connor.

"Just joking. Anyway they would have been bitten on the throat. Well that's how the legend goes."

Constable Connor stands up and knocks back the rest of his coffee.

"I know this is a wild card and probably a bit mad but contact pathology and get them to check the necks on the victims, just to see."

"OK, Constable."

Sergeant Pike leaves the office. Constable Connor picks up the report and begins re-reading it.

Carlos and Lewis are travelling in the jeep to the church to see Peter; they are already running ten minutes late.

Carlos checks his watch again and it's already 1:25 pm and they still have a short way to go.

Carlos switches on his music to listen to his favourite country CD.

"Oh Dad, not this one again."

"Hey, I thought you liked this one."

"I do but not everyday Dad. You must have other ones?"

Carlos laughs.

"OK, you win. Have a look in the glove box."

Lewis opens up the glove box, there is a half opened pack of polo mints and some tissues with lipstick blotted on them where Tanya had once put her makeup on in a rush and used the glove box as a rubbish bin, which she always used to say she was going to clear out when Carlos would moan. There was also a small collection of CDs.

Lewis gathers them all up and puts them on his lap, they are all country music except for one which was Lionel Richie's back to front album, this was Tanya's favourite.

"Can we put this one on Dad?"

Carlos looks at the CD Lewis is holding up and smiles. He leans over and roughs Lewis's hair.

"Hey. Of course. That's a good choice."

Lewis takes out the country great's album and puts in the Lionel Richie CD. It immediately begins to play.

"Ah, do it to me. Your mum loved this one."

Lewis smiled thinking of his mum, tightly holding the CD case in his hands looking at the picture of Lionel Richie on the front. Lewis turns the CD over and reads the track listing on the back.

"It seems strange coming back here so soon."

Lewis is singing along.

"Hey, are you listening?"

"Mmm?"

"I said it seems strange coming back here so soon doesn't it?"

"Do you think he has found out the truth Dad?"

They reach Church Street, and Carlos slows down as he turns the corner and looks for somewhere to park.

"Well son, let's hope he has. We'll soon find out."

Carlos parks the jeep just a short walk down from the gates. They jump out and Carlos locks it up. He puts his arm across Lewis's shoulders as they walk up to the churchyard gate.

Carlos takes a deep breath as he opens up the gate. The gate still squeaking from age.

"Oh, well here goes."

Lewis looks up at his dad.

"He didn't believe us before. He told us that, didn't he?"

"Yes true. But who knows. Let's hope, that's all we can do."

Larry is standing by a fenced off area looking up at a tree. He hears the gate close and look over and spots Carlos and Lewis entering the churchyard.

He gives them a wave as they both follow the winding path over towards him.

"Hi, Larry."

Larry looks at his watch and checks it with the church clock. It is 1:45 pm.

"Afternoon."

Larry looks quite surprised to see them both so soon after the funeral.

"Are you OK? I thought you would be at home resting; you've had quite a day of it."

Carlos snaps back.

"You mean grieving, crying into my hanky!"

Larry feels awkward.

"Oh no, I didn't mean that. I just thought…"

"It's OK, Larry. You thought it's a bit soon for me to be out and about?"

"Well, normally…"

Larry quickly stops what he was going to say and continues with a more tactful phrasing.

"Well, I'm glad you're dealing with it OK."

Carlos puts his hand on Larry's shoulder and pats it a few times.

"It's funny; when something like this happens you know you don't have a choice. You can't turn the clock back. Ain't that right son?"

Lewis agrees with a nod.

"Right, Dad."

Larry looks up at the tree again and changes the conversation trying to lighten the tone.

"I swore there was a ferret run up that tree. Now I can't see the bugger."

Lewis giggles.

"See you later, Larry. We better be off we are late for our appointment with Peter."

Lewis looks at Larry still giggling.

"See you, Larry."

Larry oblivious to Lewis and Carlos carries on muttering to himself about the ferret.

"Right you little bugger I know you're up there."

Carlos walks away towards the church, up the winding path.

***

As Carlos and Lewis enter the church, Carlos gets a chill. Peter is replacing some old candles with new.

St John's is quite a small church compared to other neighbouring villages but it is in very good condition for its five hundred and forty years.

The brass is shining bright and the wood is polished and varnished. Even the small prayer cushions of deep blue with gold trimmings are in good condition.

Large stone arches forming into perfectly formed stone pillars catching the light from the long stained glass windows.

Peter sees Carlos and Lewis.

"Ah!"

"Afternoon, Peter."

Peter puts the old candles in a cardboard box and meets Carlos and Lewis half way down the aisle.

"Sorry to ask you back here today, especially today. So soon after the funeral, I assure you it is with the utmost importance."

Peter brushes by Carlos and Lewis and walks towards the entrance carrying the box of candles.

"Come with me."

***

Larry holds up a dead rat by the tail, swinging in air.

"Another dead rat."

Larry has found seven dead rats just this morning scattered around the churchyard. Larry is quite puzzled because he hardly ever finds vermin unless they are in a trap. These rats have just been lying around on the path and around tombs and grass patches and flower beds.

Larry drops the rat into a black bag and carries on collecting litter that has blown into the churchyard from the street.

Larry walks by Tanya's freshly covered grave. He takes a double look as he passes, then walks back and stares down at the flowers.

The roses and bouquets are all brown and withered, which Larry finds impossible to believe as they have only been there for a few hours.

The funeral was at 10:15 am and it is now only 2:45 pm. How can flowers die at such a fast rate?

Larry has never seen this happen before. They look like they have been lying there for a week.

Larry picks up the dead flowers and examines them closely; there is not one alive. He throws the flowers into the black bag with the rats.

***

Peter is stood behind his desk in his study at the vicarage. Carlos and Lewis are standing in front of two comfortable soft brown leather armchairs. There are several armchairs and a couch scattered around the rather large study, all in the same soft brown leather.

The walls are made from dark wooden panels and large bookcases full of volumes of books.

Lewis is amazed by the amount; it reminds him of the library in the next village, only not nearly as big.

"Have you read them all?"

Peter looks over to Lewis and chuckles.

"I would love to say I have but the truth is I haven't. Some of them have been here before I took over the vicarage and are a few hundred years old."

Lewis's eyes widen in excitement.

"Wow."

Peter gestures towards the chairs.

"Please sit down! Make yourself comfortable."

Carlos crosses his legs.

"Well Peter, you sure do have a nice place here and only one minute from the work. I mean having a church in your front garden, now that's something!"

"Well if you put it like that, yes it is quite something."

Peter sits down in his comfortable leather office chair.

"Once again I would like to apologise for having to ask you to come back here so soon. Today especially."

Carlos's mood changes he is still touchy and upset which is normal considering the circumstances.

Carlos finishes Peter's sentence.

"Especially after burying my wife?"

"Yes. I am sorry but it is very important. The conversation yesterday about the way Tanya died."

Lewis pipes up.

"Vampires!"

Peter pauses as Carlos looks at Lewis.

"Look, let me get you both a cup of tea or coffee before we start."

Carlos looks back at Peter confused.

"Start?"

"Oh, conversation. Start our conversation"

"Oh, OK. I'll have a strong coffee and Lewis will have a tea please."

Lewis nods.

"Yes, please."

Peter has a small sink and a kettle all set up in the corner of the study. A couple of shelves above hold tins with biscuits and tea bags and coffee. Another has a row of cups and saucers and mugs.

Peter turns on the kettle and lines up three china cups; one with coffee in and two empty all standing on saucers with silver tea spoons.

The kettle boils and Peter pours the water into a silver teapot and then on the coffee in Carlos's cup. He carries Carlos's cup of coffee in one hand and a pot of tea in the other hand. He places them down on the empty desk in front of Carlos and Lewis.

"There you go; I will just get the milk."

Peter opens up a mini fridge next to the sink and takes out a small jug of milk and brings it over with Lewis's cup.

"Please, Lewis help yourself."

Peter walks back over to collect his cup.

"Do you take sugar?"

Carlos calls over to Peter.

"Yes please."

Peter brings over a bowel of sugar and his cup and saucer.

"There, help yourself."

Carlos puts one sugar in his coffee and two sugars in Lewis's tea.

Peter sits down and pours his tea.

"Now, where did we get to?"

Lewis once again pipes up.

"Vampires."

"Oh yes. Yes, well I didn't believe you and I am sorry, I should have been more sympathetic."

Carlos is a little impatient and a little short tempered and is flying off the handle at the slightest thing.

"I don't mean to be rude, Peter. But we have had quite a traumatic day and if you have brought us here to apologise for not being more understanding, more sympathetic about us being an idiot to believe in vampires then I can do without it. Especially today."

Carlos stands up.

"Come on, Lewis."

Peter stands up quickly and puts his hand out.

"No please. Let me finish. No, I didn't believe. But I had a look. I got the keys and I had a look."

Lewis jumps up.

"You found them, didn't you? They were there, weren't they?"

Carlos wipes a tear from his cheek and Peter sits back down in his chair. Carlos looks Peter in the eye and apologises for his outburst.

"I'm sorry Peter, for my explosion that's not like me it's just…"

"It's OK, Carlos. There is no need to apologise. I am the one that should be apologising. Lewis, you were right. There is something down there in the crypt."

Carlos raises his head and stares at Peter.

"You saw the vampires?"

Peter sips his tea and slumps back in his chair and exhales then pauses and shakes his head.

"God only knows what I saw. This is so hard to take in. Yes, there is something down there… they look… well I don't even know. But there are like large cocoons. Like balls, objects. They are covered in a reddish slimy liquid. They were also pulsating. They had bodies in them. There were bodies of girls lying on the floor and on the tombs. They look like they are going to give birth."

Carlos grimaces.

"Vampires?"

Peter wipes sweat from his brow with his hanky.

"Yes, I am sure they were; sharp teeth and red eyes."

Peter shouts out in anger and frustration.

"Damn their eyes staring, they saw me I'm sure of it."

Lewis looks at his dad.

"Pregnant vampires?"

"Did you recognise any of them? Did you see any of their faces?"

Peter gets up and walks over to the book case.

"Well, to be honest I didn't hang around. But there was one girl I had a proper look at. She was the girl I buried earlier this week. Susan."

Carlos turns in his chair to face Peter.

"The young girl from the post office. I didn't know she was pregnant."

Peter calmly replies to Carlos.

"She wasn't. She was the one that stared at me. I'm sure she saw me."

Lewis turns in his chair he looks at his dad and then at Peter.

"They are breeding."

Carlos quickly turns his head and looks at Lewis.

"Don't be ridiculous, that's just stupid."

Lewis suddenly stands up and moves next to Peter. He is clearly quite anxious and feels he knows more about this subject than his dad and Peter put together. After all, he has been researching it on the internet.

"Dad, this whole situation is stupid, ridiculous but it's happening, it's true. I think we are dealing with a new breed of vampire here. Who knows what they are capable of doing. And what about the cocoons? Maybe that's what they are giving birth to."

Peter pats Lewis on the head.

"Yes, I think you're right, Lewis. We must keep an open mind. Do you both need a crucifix?"

Peter walks over to a large set of mahogany draws and opens the top draw and takes out a wooden box and brings it over to his desk.

Peter opens the box and removes two crucifixes.

Lewis shakes his head.

"They won't protect you; they obviously are not affected by them. After all they are living and breeding under your church, which is full of crucifixes."

Peter is slightly taken aback when he realises the truth in what young Lewis has said. He clearly realises this lad really does know what he is talking about.

"Yes, Lewis, this is true."

Peter never thought he would ever be asking a fifteen year old advice, certainly of this nature. Peter looks at Carlos.

"So what can we use?"

"Don't look at me. Ask the expert Dr Frankenstein there."

"It's Van Helsing if you want to be accurate Dad."

116

"I stand corrected. Well, you're the one with the computer."

Carlos looks over to Peter.

"He's been looking up and researching the subject."

"I have some ideas!"

Peter and Carlos both listen to Lewis. Carlos knocks back the last of his coffee.

"We can try garlic, they are repelled by the smell of garlic; it chokes them. It might work."

"Well we have plenty of garlic in the house, Tanya used to cook with it all the time."

Lewis continues.

"Running water, holy water would be better."

Peter smirks.

"Well, I have plenty of that."

They all laugh.

Peter picks up a tray from the sink and collects the empty tea pot and cups and saucers.

"Well, that's lifted our spirits slightly, hasn't it? Anyone for another cup of tea and coffee?"

Carlos looks over his shoulder as Peter walks to the kitchen area.

"Yes. But only if you're having one?"

Peter doesn't hesitate.

"Oh yes, I am a walking tea urn!"

"So is Lewis."

"Good! I don't feel so bad now. So how can we stop them? I've seen a few of the films. A wooden stake in the heart? Decapitation?"

Lewis sits back down in the chair and turns to face Peter.

"Maybe? But we don't know. We should take another look at them and roughly work out how many we are dealing with."

There is a knock on the study door. Peter calls out from the kitchen sink.

"Come in."

The door opens slowly and Larry pokes his head around and looks around. He then walks in and half closes the door.

"Sorry to disturb you. But can I have a word in private, Peter?"

Larry leaves the room and Peter follows glancing at Carlos.

"Excuse me."

"No problem."

Carlos shouts through the closed study door.

"I'll finish the tea and coffee."

***

Larry stood in the hall glancing up at one of the few portraits hung in the long hallway of the vicarage, all dating back a few hundred years, with oils that had cracked in places over time.

Peter shut the door behind him, leaving Carlos to make the coffee and tea.

Larry was fiddling with his fingers, which was a sure sign that he was nervous about something.

"What is it, Larry?"

"Well, I had to come and see you, it's so strange."

"What's happened?"

"Those flowers on Tanya's grave; they are all dead."

118

Peter went quiet while he was thinking.

"Dead?"

Larry agrees wiping his hands down his side.

"Every single one. All dried up like a two month old rose."

"But that's impossible."

"All of them, Peter."

"But they are all fresh. They can't have been on the grave more than a few hours."

Larry pulls back his sleeve and looks at his watch.

"The funeral was 11:15 am and the time is now 3:05 pm. That makes it three hours and fifty minutes to be exact."

Peter spreads his fingers across his brow as he tries to think. Larry continues to explain.

"Yes, they were fresh just under four hours ago, but now they look like they've been dead for two months. Very strange."

"Just put them in the bin and don't say anything to anyone."

"I have already."

"Good."

Larry suddenly looks up directly at Peter.

"What if Carlos asks about his flowers?"

"Leave it with me."

Peter reassures Larry by patting him on the back.

"You don't know anything until I tell you. OK?"

"OK. You know best. I just thought you should know, that's all."

"No, I am glad you told me. I will see you later."

Peter walks Larry back to the open front door; Peter always keeps it open when he is in, to let the fresh air in. He watches Larry wander off back through the church yard. As Peter walks back to the door to the study, he thinks to himself how he is going to break this. Especially as Carlo is very touchy at the moment.

***

He enters the study and closes the door behind him.

Peter sits down in his chair. Carlos and Lewis staring, noticing Peter was feeling uncomfortable.

Suddenly Peter stands up and smiles trying to lighten the atmosphere.

"Drink?"

Lewis points to the cup and saucer and the fresh pot of tea standing on the desk waiting.

"Of course."

Peter begins to pour. Carlos notices that Peter is shaking slightly.

"Everything OK, Peter?"

"Yes, yes yes."

"OK."

Peter takes a sip of his tea and remembers he hasn't put a sugar in it as he pulls a face.

"Sugar."

Peter puts one sugar in the cup and stirs it.

"Look. Yes, I'm just a bit baffled... You might as well know as it looks like we're in this together."

Peter sits forward and looks Carlos straight in the eye.

"The flower's on your wife's grave."

"What about them?"

Lewis looks at Carlos waiting for him to lose his temper.

"They are all dead. That's what Larry has just told me."

"What? Dead? How?"

Lewis looks at Carlos then Peter,

"It's starting to happen."

Carlos jumps at Lewis.

"What's starting to happen?"

Lewis takes a sip of his tea carefully blowing on it first to cool it slightly.

"It's all part of the turning process. Mum was bitten by a vampire and she died by the bite of a vampire."

Carlos continues the sentence guessing the answer.

"So, she will become a vampire?"

Lewis agrees.

"Yes, Dad. There is nothing we can do."

Peter looks wide eyed at Carlos, almost slight panic written across both of their faces as Lewis explains.

"In the old times, they had horses to jump over graves to find a vampire. The horse wouldn't jump over a vampire's grave. The grave always had dead flowers or no flowers on it. Nothing will grow above the sleeping place of a vampire. That's how they could tell."

Peter sits back in his chair.

"Well, Lewis you certainly have done your homework."

Carlos looks at Peter.

"So, what can we do?"

Peter shakes his head.

"What can we do?"

Peter looks at Lewis.

"I don't know. I wish I did. What do you think, Lewis?"

"She will probably turn into a vampire tonight."

Carlos slumps back into his chair.

Chapter Eighteen

The clouds are starting to form across the pale blue sky. The sun seems to dart in and out of the clouds casting a multitude of shadows across the ground, from the surrounding trees and buildings in the village.

The main street is quiet, just a few cars parked up along the designated curbs and very little traffic.

Mrs Brown is chatting on the doorstep of the convenience store with a customer, no doubt getting all the latest gossip. As Constable Connor and Sergeant Pike drive by, she spots them and waves. Sergeant Pike waves back and smiles.

"Mrs Brown looks busy collecting more gossip, no doubt."

Constable Connor nods his head.

"Or giving them a rundown on today's events."

Sergeant Pike raises his eyebrows.

"The funeral."

"Yep."

Sergeant Pike takes an apple out from his pocket and rubs it on his lapel until it shines, he takes a long hard look at it.

"It looks like one of them wax ones now, doesn't it?"

Constable Connor continues driving and concentrating on the road.

"Eh? Wax what?"

"It looks like a wax one."

Sergeant Pike holds up the apple in front of Constable Connor.

"Look."

Constable Connor just tuts and shakes his head.

"Oh, just eat it."

Sergeant Pike smiles, then takes a large bite out of the rosy side of the apple, it makes a loud crunch. The juice runs down his chin.

"Juicy."

"Sorry, what was that you sprayed?"

Sergeant Pike chuckles as he chews away, then swallows wiping his mouth with a tissue which he kept in his pocket.

"Did you manage to get hold of Carlos then?"

Constable Connor glances over while Sergeant Pike wipes his lips with the tissue.

"Well, I did try but there was no answer. He was probably lying down after the funeral. Emotionally drained, I would imagine."

Sergeant Pike agrees.

"Yes, you are probably right."

Constable Connor pulls up outside Carlos's home.

"Let's hope he's up and about."

They both get out of the car and walk up to the front door. Sergeant Pike looks at Constable Connor.

"Shall I do the honour?"

"Just knock."

Sergeant Pike raps the brass door knocker. They wait until the door opens. Carlos is still in his funeral clothes.

"Constable, Sergeant!"

Constable Connor smiles at Carlos.

"Carlos, good afternoon, I hope you don't mind us dropping in but we were in the area and thought we would give you a call."

Carlos opens the door to invite them in.

"Come in."

"Thank you."

Carlos closes the door.

"Go on through."

They all enter the living room. Lewis is sat on the sofa reading a book titled The Factual History of Vampires, one of many he has in his collection.

"That's very thoughtful. Well you have only just caught us, we have been out all day."

"Yes. That's one of the reasons we wanted to come by and say hello."

Constable Connor smiles at Lewis as he looks up from his book.

"Hi!"

"Hello, Lewis. I wanted to apologise for not being at the funeral. Heavy workload held us back."

Carlos politely agrees, knowing full well they weren't exactly inundated at the station with work. Nothing much ever happens here in this village.

"Lewis, would you mind making a pot of coffee please?"

Lewis jumps up and lays his book on the coffee table.

"Oh sorry, please have a seat."

"You've met Pike before, haven't you?"

"Yes, a few times I believe."

Carlos steps forward and bends down to shake Pikes hand while he is sat in an armchair.

Constable Connor sits down on another sofa, admiring the large open inglenook fireplace.

There is chopped wood piled up on the hearth and brass tongs, poker, brush and shovel hanging on an ornate stand on both sides. A large shelf above the fireplace, decorated with rows of elephants and a few photographs in frames.

Everything in the living room looked clean and well kept. Colour coordinated from curtains in burgundy, matching cushions right down to the material which stand out vividly against the cream sofas.

Constable Connor looks up at Carlos.

"I hope it all went smoothly for you today, Carlos."

"It went as well as to be expected. A lot of flowers. Well there were until… well, anyway it doesn't matter. You said there was something else you wanted to discuss with me?"

Sergeant Pike looks at Constable Connor awaiting a response.

"Did I?"

"Well, you didn't actually say there was something else. You said one of the reasons you came was to apologise for not coming to the funeral. So what was the other reason?"

Sergeant Pike laughs.

"He's got you there constable."

Sergeant Pike continues to chuckle to himself.

"You should be a policeman! Yes, it's rather a difficult one really."

Sergeant Pike uncrosses his legs and looks towards Constable Connor, then he gets up and walks over to the fireplace and admires the elephants lined up on the shelf.

Sergeant Pike picks up one of the elephants and explains.

"Well, we had tests done on the bodies."

Carlos looks shocked. Just as Carlos was going to raise his voice, Lewis walks in with a pot of coffee and some mugs, milk and sugar on a tray.

Lewis places the tray on the coffee table and begins to pour out the coffee.

Carlos looks at Constable Connor.

"Bodies? What bodies?"

Lewis calls out to everyone.

"OK, who is for sugar and who isn't? OK, Dad you don't have sugar."

Sergeant Pike answers for both of them.

"We both take two. Thanks, Lewis."

"So, tell me what about the bodies?"

"Recently you must have been aware of the amount of strange deaths we have had in the village?"

"Well, I knew there were some deaths and quite a few close together but I didn't think it was strange to be honest. Well, not until now that you mention it."

Constable Connors cuts in as Sergeant Pike sits down to drink his coffee.

"Forensics always look at the bodies, especially in strange circumstances to determine cause of death. All the results came back the same for each body including your wife. All had nearly half their blood missing."

Lewis looks up after blowing on his coffee.

"Did you find the bite marks?"

Sergeant Pike looks directly at Constable Connor who then looks at Carlos.

"Well, we did find something."

Lewis adds very confidently.

"On the throat? Two puncture marks on the jugular vein."

"Yes, how did you know?"

"It's how a vampire feeds."

Constable Connor gives himself a reality check but brushes it off as nonsense.

"Oh come on! Vampires? Don't be ridic…"

Carlos cuts in raising his voice.

"Now, just hold on."

Constable Connor sits back in his chair.

"Constable, you should listen to what Lewis has got to say. Seriously."

"Yes, but vampires. That's just taking it a little too far."

Sergeant Pike adds to the conversation and brings up an issue that Constable Connor wasn't ready to discuss.

"What about the empty graves, constable?"

Constable Connor turns and grits his teeth at Pike.

"Pike!"

"Well, it's true. What about them? It sort of makes sense, doesn't it?"

Carlos questions Constable Connor,

"Empty graves?"

Constable Connor nods his head.

"Yes, empty graves."

Once again Sergeant Pike gets up from his armchair and moves next to Constable Connor.

"So far all the bodies we have done tests on have disappeared from their graves except…"

Carlos quickly interrupts.

"Tanya's?"

Constable Connor lowers his head and nods his head once more thinking this is one of the hardest days in his career.

"Yes. Tanya's."

"Mum was bitten by a vampire and killed by a vampire."

Constable Connor sits up in his chair.

"What?"

"I have seen them with Dad."

Constable Connor stands up and walks around to the back of his chair.

"But this is unbelievable. Vampires here in Cornwall?"

Carlos walks over to Constable Connor.

"It's true. Even the vicar has seen them."

"The vicar?"

"Yes, constable."

Lewis interjects.

"I have an idea. If you don't believe us and you need proof, then we should watch Mum's grave. She will rise tonight as a vampire."

Sergeant Pike stares at Carlos.

"This sounds crazy."

Carlos starts to get a little het up.

"It is crazy. But it is also true and when you see for yourself, you will believe. Then maybe we can sit down and fathom a way of destroying these things."

Constable Connor sits back down and finishes his coffee, then looks up at Carlos after an awkward silence.

"Well, I don't know."

Constable thinks for a few seconds while all eyes looking at him, waiting for him to say something.

"Did you say the vicar has seen them?"

Lewis looks at Constable Connor.

"Yes, he has. He is joining us tonight."

"Well OK. But if you're wrong I'll…"

Carlos butts in and finishes off the sentence as to how he imagined it to be.

"Have us sectioned? Well, we will give you permission. Is that a deal?"

Constable Connor nods then looks over to Sergeant Pike who nods back.

"OK. What time?"

"11:30 pm. That gives us time to find a good spot."

"I can't believe what I'm saying or even agreeing to. This has to be strictly between us, OK? I'm putting my neck on the line here."

"Probably not the best choice of words, constable."

Constable Connor questions Sergeant Pike with one of his looks.

"Your neck, constable. On the line. Vampires like a bit of neck."

"Oh, shut up."

Lewis giggles looking up at Carlos.

Chapter Nineteen

Peter is standing outside of the churchyard waiting for Carlos, Lewis, Constable Connor and Sergeant Pike to show. The night is quite cool and it's rather misty in patches, which are fairly normal for this part of the coast, this time of year.

Peter spots Carlos's jeep approaching the church followed by Constable Connor and Sergeant Pike in their car. Carlos waves to Peter as he locks up the jeep. Lewis runs up the path and stands alongside Peter, he looks up and smiles.

"Hello, Lewis, I bet you're tired."

"No, not really."

"Oh, that's good because it could be a long night."

Carlos is followed by Constable Connor and Sergeant Pike.

"Good evening, Peter."

"Good evening!"

Connor and Pike both speak in unison.

"Evening."

Carlos and Lewis, open the gate to the church yard. It still manages to squeak, which somehow seems so much louder in the night air.

"Damn gate."

Carlos and Lewis are followed by the vicar, Connor and Pike. They all stop as Pike closes the gate.

"Needs a drop of oil I think."

Peter suggests they hide behind the bushes that are closest to Tanya's grave, pointing out the options. Pike looks a little nervous.

"Well, maybe we could watch a bit further back just in case."

Connor suddenly looks at Pike with one of his stares.

"Just in case what?"

Peter gulps nervously.

"Well, just in case they're hungry."

Carlos interrupts Connor before he gets into a full blown bickering match.

"No, I think you're right, Peter. We need to be as close as possible so we can see, especially as its getting misty out here tonight."

They all head over to a decent size bush where they can all quite comfortably watch behind. Peter stops.

"Right here is the best spot, I think. Agreed?"

The ground is cold and slightly damp as they all sit down trying to make themselves as comfortable as they can.

"What time is it?"

Carlos rolls his shirt sleeve up just enough to look at his watch.

"11:40 pm."

Connor shakes his head and point up to the church tower.

"Haven't you notice the lovely big clock on the church?"

"Oh, I never thought I was concentrating. It seems to be going so slow."

"We have only just got here Pike, how can it be going slow. I sometimes think you're the only one that's slow around here."

***

Fresh untouched soil lay neatly in a long and narrow mound as mist swirls around Tanya's grave.

The black marble headstone catches the moon light through the tall yew trees. The churchyard is deadly quiet as the clock passes 12:00 am, not a sound, not even an owl.

Small balls of soil roll gently down on Tanya's grave as the ground begins to vibrate.

Suddenly, there is a loud bang as soil is flung high into the air followed by the coffin lid leaving an open grave.

Carlos stands up as everyone else jumps.

Carlos speaks in a loud whisper.

"Fuck, did you see that."

Tanya's body lay cold and still. Her face like wax; her lips still red from the lipstick, that the cosmetologist had put on, standing out against her white skin.

Tanya's eyes suddenly opened, the whites of her eyes are blood red, her body trembles then she elevates into the upright position without bending her legs.

As she reaches ground level and turns her head sharply, with her eyes wide open she snarls at the night sky like an animal about to hunt.

Constable Connor is in total shock.

"Fuck."

Carlos feels sick as he sees what his beautiful wife Tanya has turned into. He turns his head and closes his eyes as he wants to scream out. Lewis runs to his dad and hugs him tightly. Peter crosses himself uttering the Lord's Prayer under his breath. Eventually they all settle down into comfortable positions behind the bush and watch Tanya walk over to the church.

Pike attempts to speak and Connor hushes him.

"Just be quiet. Just watch!"

Tanya stops in her tracks as she reaches the church then puts both hands on the wall of the church. Her fingers spread wide as they begin to change. Her fingers elongate and appear hook liked at the tips.

Slowly Tanya begins to climb the clock tower of the church. Her talons grabbing and hooking into and onto every stone as she makes her way high up past the clock and onto the dark slate roof of St John's.

Pike looks at Peter wide eyed and wide mouthed.

"What the hell?"

All watching waiting but not knowing what they are waiting for. Tanya stands up on the roof, she snarls at the moon then bends her legs and leaps high up into the sky, her arms and legs stretched out she transforms in a large bat. She swoops low across the treetops heading towards the village.

Constable Connor shakes his head in bewilderment. Lewis and Carlos still holding each other tightly not believing what they have just seen; Pike sits down and buries his head in his hands.

Peter looks over to Carlos and Lewis to make sure they are OK. Connor puts his hands on his hips and chews his bottom lip.

"Excuse me, Peter but what the fuck is going on?"

Lewis wipes his eyes where he had been secretly crying.

"Vampires. We told you. Now do you believe us?"

Constable Connor relaxes.

"Well yes. But how? And why here?"

Peter shrugs his shoulders.

"God only knows."

Carlos is listening to the conversation but at the same time watching the church, he notices something strange at the bottom of the crypt door.

"Quick, look! The crypt."

Everyone looks over to the crypt and feasts their eyes on the door. The stones under the bottom of the large old wooden door have been worn away with time and years of constant use. Three very clear lines of mist slowly seep out from under the door climbing up over the door and onto the wall of the church.

The mist climbs up until it reaches the top of the clock tower. Shapes start to form from the mist into three female figures that turn into bats as they leap high into the air and fly off swooping low across the trees towards the village.

Peter pats Carlos on the back and addresses everyone.

"Come on. Let's all go to the vicarage. We have seen enough. We need to discuss what we need to do next."

Sergeant Pike agrees with a quick nod of the head.

"Good idea."

Carlos looks at everyone and puts his arm across Lewis's shoulder.

"I really need to go home. I'm so tired."

Lewis looks up at Carlos.

"No, Dad. Not home. It might not be safe. What if Mum returns home? If she does and we are there, it will be because she needs blood. It won't be to see how we are. She will only want to feed."

"Feed?"

Lewis answers Constable Connor.

"Yes, feed. They drink your blood with one bite but can kill you with a different bite. It's usually called the kiss of death."

Pike shakes his head in disbelief.

"Sounds a bit corny."

"It's what I have read. That's what it is referred to as."

"So if I get bitten I won't turn into a vampire?"

Lewis shakes his head.

"No, not straight away. Not unless they just want to feed and then kill which does happen a lot. Otherwise, it's a slow death until the end. The final bite can be savage."

"Throats being ripped open, that sort of thing."

Pike holds his throat and Connor looks at Pike. Connor clears his throat to speak.

"I wonder if that's what killed the three chaps in the lighthouse? They were in a bit of a mess."

Peter stretches his arms out as to round his flock up.

"Come on, let's get back to the vicarage and get a cup of tea and coffee."

Pike looks straight at Peter.

"After all that, I think we could do with something a bit stronger."

Constable Connor agrees.

"On this occasion, Pike. I think I have to agree."

Peter smiles.

"Come on then, I'm sure I can find you all something."

Everyone follows Peter across the grass and back onto the path in the churchyard. Pike and Connor keep checking behind them making sure nothing is following them. Lewis spots them.

"I don't think you need to worry. They will be in the village by now."

They continue up the path following Peter to the vicarage.

Chapter Twenty

The crypt is dark with only a small long narrow window with broken glass letting light in through the cobwebs. Year ago the window would have been stained glass held in by lead but now it's just jagged, broken fragments held together by cobwebs and dust.

There are several pillars standing along the centre of the crypt with large concrete tombs lined up along the walls and several that stand in the centre.

The stone is dusty and has discoloured with age, once upon a time probably almost white but now very grey and chipped. The ceiling is almost black with dirt and shadow and large cobwebs hanging down collecting dust.

The light shard through the broken window, made up from the light of the moon, picks out the dust floating in the air.

A vine has crept in from the window and down the wall, feeling its way towards a pillar.

Lying on several tombs are bodies of young woman; naked and pregnant. Some only just showing, others huge, bigger than normal.

A young woman is lit only by the shard of light coming from the window. Her body is pale and clammy, her eyes are open and blood red, her fangs biting the air as if she is trying to catch insects; groaning and snarling.

Her stomach is moving and swelling. Suddenly, it splits open, almost down to her vagina. There is very little blood but brown and dark red ooze or slime falls to the floor carrying a pulsating transparent ball.

The vampire lying on the tomb lays still and her stomach begins to heal in minutes; joining up as if nothing ever happened. She closes her eyes and takes a big gasp of air and rests.

The slime from the ball drips to the floor revealing a cocoon shaped egg, transparent with a human body inside. The cocoon grows quite rapidly; already doubled in size in just a short while.

There are several cocoons lying around the crypt floor.

One is huge, almost as high as the tomb, which it is lying next to.

It is completely transparent and clearly there is a naked female inside. It pulsates for a few minutes and the girl inside opens her eyes. They are blood red.

The cocoon splits open and the naked woman stands up. Her body pale, her hair dark her, eyes red and her fangs are long and sharp as she snarls.

Two more cocoons open revealing two more naked female vampires.

Chapter Twenty-One

Sergeant Pike closes the vicarage door behind him as he is the last to enter into the hallway. As he follows everyone else, he checks out the old oil paintings. He thinks that they look a little out of place in such a narrow hall and would be the sort of picture you would find in a large country manor or a castle somewhere.

The wall lights are dim with an orange glow, behind frosted glass that barely lights anything at all.

Following through into the lounge, Lewis has already claimed a corner of the sofa and Carlos an armchair. Peter notices them all looking at the seats.

"Don't worry, there are plenty of chairs about the room, just pull up a couple if you prefer."

Constable Connor pulls up an armchair and Pike chooses another armchair.

Peter gently claps his hands.

"Right, drinks?"

Carlos puts his hand up as a gesture of agreement and Pike questions.

"What do you have, Peter?"

"Well, there is tea or coffee or wine or brandy if you prefer?"

Constable Connor suddenly opens his eyes after a few seconds of rest.

"Ahh, brandy now that sounds like a nice idea. Could I have it with a coffee?"

Pike looks directly at Connor.

"Hey, that's a cheek."

Peter laughs.

"No, don't you worry its quite normal, that is what I have of an evening."

"Well, then I will have the same."

Carlos nods.

"Make that three."

Carlos gets up, "Can I give you a hand, Peter?"

"Thank you, now what about you, Lewis?"

"Just a tea please, Peter."

Carlos and Peter head for the kitchen. Peter switches on the kettle and Carlos sorts out the glasses and mugs.

Carlos looks at Peter and smiles.

"Peter, does this feel like a dream to you?"

"Yes it does, but I can assure you it's not."

"Yes, I know that but I just feel like, please let me wake up. This just cannot be happening."

Constable Connor overhears, "In all the years I've been working as a constable and in the forces, I have never witnessed anything like it."

Lewis chirps up crossing his arms smiling,

"Yeah, vampires don't come about every day."

Everyone laughs.

Carlos laughing, looks over to Lewis who is quite pleased with himself for making people laugh.

"Well son, that lightened the spirit a bit."

Pike stretches his neck, round the wings of his armchair, looking towards the kitchen.

"Talking of spirits."

Constable Connor cuts in staring at Pike.

"No ghost stories, Pike."

"I was going to say talking of spirits, is the brandy on its way?"

Carlos laughs.

"Yep, it's on its way. Just getting the coffee on the tray and I'll be right over."

Peter puts the last mug and the sugar on the tray and follows Carlos over to the chairs. Carlos puts the tray down onto the large coffee table. He takes Lewis's tea and places it in front of him.

"Right, guys help yourself."

Carlos points to the cups and glasses.

"Coffee, sugar, milk, brandy, help yourself."

Peter sits himself at his desk in his super soft and comfortable leather office chair. He takes a sip of his brandy and lets out a gasp of warm air and smiles.

"Now that is what the doctor ordered."

He looks at everyone sipping their tea, coffee and brandy.

"Right, everyone now we are all comfortable and we have our beverages. We need to continue our discussion."

Carlos nods.

"Agreed."

Constable Connor raises his glass.

"So, what are we dealing with?"

Pike looks at Connor with an 'I don't believe you even said that' look. "Vampires!"

"I know that. But I mean how dangerous, how are we going to stop them?"

Shaking his head Sergeant Pike looks at everyone.

"They kill; I think that is dangerous enough."

Peter leans forward in his chair.

"Clearly this is a new strain. A new type of vampire. There have been stories of vampires going back centuries. Some never proven, others well, still in doubt. But in the church we cannot be seen to believe in such things."

"But you do now?"

"Yes sergeant, I do."

Peter stands up to address everyone as if he was in his church addressing his flock.

"Those things are breeding."

"But why?"

"Who knows, Carlos? I can only assume they are a dying race. They probably have to reproduce to survive. I don't know, that's my only conclusion."

Carlos sighs nodding slowly.

"I guess it makes sense."

Connor slaps his leg and pushes himself back into the chair.

"So they've decided to breed here in Cornwall. Great!"

Peter stands up straight, his mood changes. Everyone stops and watches as he pauses.

"If we don't stop them before those things hatch, we could be faced with a plague of them, an army. None of us would survive that."

Pike sits forward.

"How many are there, down there?"

"I didn't count but probably ten or more. It was too dark and I didn't hang around to count."

Peter sits back down and knocks the rest of the brandy back and lets out a small gasp of air.

Constable Connor rubs the back of his neck and stretches his arms out.

"OK so, what do you suggest?"

Connor yawns and Pike watches.

"We could go into the crypt and put a couple of wooden stakes into the hearts and see if that works."

Lewis watches and listens to the conversation just waiting for an opportunity to butt in.

Connor sits up in his chair then stands up, stretching his legs.

"Are you serious?"

Carlos interrupts.

"That's way too dangerous."

Sergeant Pike stands up facing Constable Connor.

"You got any better ideas?"

"Look guys, we don't know if wooden stakes work and if they don't well…"

Connor finishes Carlos's sentence.

"They are going to get pissed off."

Carlos agrees looking at Lewis. Lewis nods his head.

"Yeah, big time."

Peter stands holding up his brandy glass.

"Anyone for a refill?"

Everyone agrees.

"Would you like another tea, Lewis?"

"Yes please."

Peter switches the kettle on in the kitchenette and brings over the half empty bottle of brandy to the table.

Carlos collects all the mugs.

Peter calls over.

"Would you like another coffee to go with your brandy?"

Everyone agrees that would be a good idea.

Once everyone is settled back down in their chairs and Pike and Connor have finished stretching their legs. Lewis has found a history book on St John's Church and is busy reading up on the history.

The conversation begins again with Pike, "This reproduction thing. I still don't get it!"

Peter moves over to his office chair and sits down answering Pike,

"I don't think any of us do. One thing I do know. That girl Susan wasn't pregnant when she was buried this week and when I saw her in the crypt, she looked ready to give birth to an elephant."

"How come?"

Lewis looks up from his book obviously keeping one ear open for a chance to join in the conversation.

"Breeding."

"Exactly, Lewis. They obviously can reproduce and give birth in weeks, maybe days to those cocoons. Some of them cocoons are massive, I believe they continue to grow after they have left the body."

Lewis puts his book down onto the table.

"We could do a test?"

"A test, what sort of test?"

Lewis elaborates.

"Holy water. We can pour some holy water into the empty graves of the vampires and see if it burns. If it does, it will do the same to them."

Carlos pats Lewis on the back and rubs his shoulder.

"Good thinking, son."

Peter agrees.

"First thing in the morning, we will try. It's too dangerous now."

Lewis agrees yawning. Peter notices Pike watching Lewis yawn then join in.

"I can see we are all very tired. Let's try and get some sleep. I'll go and fetch some blankets. You can all sleep in here for tonight. If you need refreshments, you know where the tea and coffee is."

Peter leaves the room and Carlos stretches out on the sofa with Lewis, while Sergeant Pike and Constable Connor find a couple of pouffes to rest their feet on as they lounge in their armchairs. Peter enters the room carrying a pile of blankets.

"Here we go, blankets for everyone."

Peter shares them all out before leaving the room.

Chapter Twenty-Two

St Paul's Church is only lit by the moon. The sky is clear and the stars clearly seen twinkling above in the night sky.

The mist is thinning out around the church and the gravestones and tombs can now clearly be seen.

The green of the trees and bushes and grass can be seen in between the dark shadows lit by the moon.

There is silence. Not a bird or even vermin can be heard. Nothing just peace and quiet.

In the distance, four figures appear. As they slowly walk closer, the moonlight shows they are completely naked. Tanya with three other vampires.

Their skin is as white as snow, their eyes burning red and fangs as sharp as razors.

Blood has run down the sides of their mouths and in between their breasts.

As they reach the crypt door, they all stop and stand in a row looking up at the church. One by one they begin to dissolve into mist and seep under the crypt door.

Chapter Twenty-Three

Peter returns from the hall carrying two newspapers which he has delivered every day. Peter likes to be kept up-to-date with the news. He lays them on the table and whispers across to Constable Connor.

"If you fancy a read, I'll leave them here."

He looks across to Sergeant Pike who smiles and nods, still wiping sleep from his eyes with his hanky.

Constable Connor picks up a newspaper and unfolds it.

"The daily echo, well let's see what crap they have printed in it today."

Peter looks over from the kitchenette.

Sergeant Pike creeps around the room, he looks over to Carlos who is still asleep; Lewis is sitting drinking a cup of tea.

"Would you like some help, Peter?"

"No, you are OK. I'm just making your tea. You can sit down. I'll bring it over in a sec."

"OK."

Peter pours the hot water into the pot and gives it a few stirs with the spoon then shuts the lid and pours out the tea into four mugs. He wanders over with the tray and puts it down on the table. After picking up a mug, he taps Carlos on the shoulder. Carlos jumps.

"Mmm. Yes what?"

Carlos looks at Peter through blurry eyes and waits for his eyes to focus. Peter is holding a mug of tea in his hand.

"A mug of tea for you, Carlos."

Carlos sits up scratching the back of his head and yawns again. His eyes focus on Peter's hand holding out a mug.

"Thank you!"

Peter passes the mug over so Carlos can take hold of the handle.

"Sorry to wake you, Carlos but we need to do the test on Tanya's grave."

Carlos still sleepy blows onto the hot mug of tea before he takes a sip.

"Test?"

Carlos thinks for a second then remembers.

"Oh yes, the test. What time is it?"

Lewis watching his dad waking up is a normal thing. He is used to seeing his dad like this.

Every weekend when he doesn't have to work, Carlos always has a lay in and Lewis takes him up a hot cup of coffee.

So Lewis doesn't see anything different in today other than that Carlos is drinking tea and not coffee and he is waking up in a vicarage on a sofa and not his own bed.

Lewis checks his wrist watch.

"10:15 am, Dad."

Carlos realises where he is and what's going on. He smiles at his son and ruffles Lewis's hair.

"Ah, Lewis. Are you OK, son?"

"Yes, Dad. I'm fine. You should drink your tea."

Carlos rubs his forehead.

"I've got a bit of a thick head. I must have slept heavy."

Peter pats him on the shoulder and walks off reassuring him.

"Well, you did have a bit of a heavy day yesterday."

Sergeant smiles and adds to Peters comment.

"And the brandy probably didn't help; we have almost polished off a bottle between us."

Carlos looks up and remembers.

"Damn, really? I guess you could be right then."

Peter notices Constable Connor collecting the empty brandy glasses and mugs from the table.

"There's no need to do that, constable. I can do that later."

He takes them to the kitchenette and puts them into the sink as Peter watches.

"Habit, Peter. You get used to doing it when you live alone."

Carlos looks at Lewis and they both smile. Carlos knocks back the rest of his tea.

"OK Mum, I'm done. You can take this one too."

The joke goes right over Constable Connor's head. Pike chuckles and even Peter smiles. Connor has his hands in the sink, his sleeves rolled up washing the glasses.

"Leave it there, I've only got one pair of hands."

He holds one up to the light after rinsing it in cold water.

"Now that's how you do it, that's how you get the sparkle back in the glass."

Carlos laughs and Lewis, Pike and Peter join in. Connor is oblivious to what anyone is laughing at and just carries on in his own little world.

Peter collects two small glass bottles, no bigger than small perfume bottles, made of tinted glass from a draw in the study of the vicarage. He puts them in his pocket.

"OK, let us meet outside the church doors in ten minutes or so, I just have to collect the holy water."

Chapter Twenty-Four

Peter walks slowly down the aisle of St John's Church. He looks high up at the beautiful stained glass windows that tower up each side of him, making up a large story across and around the church walls.

The light hitting the glass from the outside brightens the darkest colours on the glass and makes them shine across the church.

Peter reaches the front; he puts his hand in his pocket and pulls out the two small bottles. Carefully standing one bottle on the ledge, he unscrews the lid from the other then fills up the bottle to the brim. He carefully screws back on the lid and repeats the process with the other bottle.

After placing both bottles in his pocket, he bows to the cross, crossing himself. He then walks back up the aisle and out through the church door.

Connor, Pike, Carlos and Lewis are all waiting as planned, just outside the old wooden church doors.

As Peter leaves the church, he closes the door and locks it behind him. Pike is always quick to try and lighten the mood.

"All set, vicar. Armed and dangerous?"

Peter on this occasion isn't amused and chooses to ignore Pike's childish comment. Peter has more worrying things on his mind at present and could probably do without Pike's humour at this moment in time.

He realises it was the wrong thing to say and looks down quite embarrassed.

Constable Connor also isn't amused and tries to smooth things over.

"Glad you're finding all of this amusing, Pike."

"I'm only trying to lighten things up a bit."

Carlos interjects.

"It's OK, Constable."

Lewis gets out of the way and runs up to walk alongside Peter, who is a quite few paces in front of everyone else.

"Are you OK, Lewis?"

"Yes I'm OK. Can I ask you a question?"

Peter looks down to Lewis.

"Yes, of course you can."

"How do you get the water to be holy? Is it just with the prayer?"

Peter smiles and puts his hand on Lewis's shoulder as they walk. Lewis notices the warmth of Peter's hand radiating through his clothes and onto his shoulder.

"Yes, just a prayer and from the help of an old friend of ours up there."

Peter gestures with his head glancing up to the sky.

Lewis looks up to the sky too.

"Oh, right."

Peter and Lewis reach Tanya's grave first, followed by Carlos, then a few paces behind Constable Connor and Sergeant Pike.

Carlos and Lewis move around to one side of the grave, leaving Connor and Pike on the opposite side, while Peter stands at the foot of the grave.

They all look down in disbelief into Tanya's empty coffin.

Peter dressed in his proper attire of robes and ribbons. He pulls out the bible, there is a book mark with a red ribbon attached, hanging from the appropriate page.

He opens up the Bible and looks around at everyone.

Carlos gulps and holds Lewis's hand.

"Are we ready?"

Everyone nods their heads.

"Then I shall begin. I will require absolute silence while I read this prayer."

Carlos looks at Lewis while Connor looks at Pike. Peter once again looks at everyone before looking back down at the Bible to read.

Peter crosses himself.

"Most glorious Prince of the Heavenly Armies, St Michael the Archangel, defend us in 'our battle against principalities and powers, against the rulers of this world of darkness, against the spirits of wickedness in the high places'. Come to the assistance of men who God has created to His likeness and whom He has redeemed at a great price from the tyranny of the devil. Holy Church venerates thee as her guardian and protector; to thee, the Lord has entrusted the souls of the redeemed to be led into heaven. Pray therefore the God of Peace to crush Satan beneath our feet, that he may no longer retain men captive and do injury to the Church. Offer our prayers to the Most High, that without delay they may draw His mercy down upon us; take hold of 'the dragon, the old serpent, which is the devil and Satan', bind him and cast him into the bottomless pit so that he may no longer seduce the nations."

Peter takes out from his pocket a small bottle of holy water. He unscrews the lid from the bottle and makes the sign of the cross with the holy water into the empty coffin.

The water burns through the coffin in the sign of the cross like acid on plastic. Melting and carving the holy symbol forever in Tanya's place of rest.

Carlos turns his head. Lewis looks up at Peter and Pike looks at Constable Connor and shivers.

"Good God."

Connor also looks at Peter for answers.

"Peter, now what?"

"We need to think. We all need to think very hard about what we can do. Clearly holy water is the only thing that has proven to work. I suggest we all go away and have a think. I am busy for the next few days, I have a few services and burials to attend to, so let us meet back here in three days. I'm here if you need me."

Carlos nods in agreement.

"OK, let's do that."

Sergeant Pike and Constable Connor both shake Peter's hand.

"See you shortly and thank you for your help; we are going to need it."

"Yes, Constable, and may God help us."

Connor and Pike walk off leaving Carlos and Lewis standing alone. They watch them heading down the path and out of sight.

Peter looks at Carlos and Lewis and smiles. He watches Carlos turn to leave with Lewis, as he does he puts his hand into his pocket then quickly he calls out.

"Carlos."

As Carlos and Lewis turn back and walk over towards Peter. Peter takes out from his pocket a small bottle of holy water and gives it to Carlos.

"Here, take this for your protection, you may need it."

Carlos looks down at the small glass bottle in his hand.

"It's holy water."

Carlos takes another look.

"Thank you, Peter."

Lewis looks up at Peter and smiles.

"Thank you."

Carlos puts his arm around Lewis's shoulders and directs him to the path.

"Take care, Peter."

Peter smiles and watches them both disappear out of sight.

"May God protect you."

Chapter Twenty-Five

Well everything had been very quiet for couple of days and Carlos and Lewis had managed to catch up on some much needed sleep. The bags and dark rings had disappeared from Carlos's eyes and he looked as fresh and handsome as Tanya always liked him.

Lewis finished his studying for his school exams, not that he was back at school yet. The school had advised Carlos to maybe keep him out from school for a couple of weeks, until he had got over the shock of losing his mum.

Carlos agreed as he also had taken a couple of weeks off work.

Today the sun was shining through Lewis's bedroom window while he sat at his computer scrolling and surfing the net, researching as much information about vampires. Carlos was in the back garden cutting the grass. He always liked a tidy garden and Tanya would often help him plant her favourite flowers. All of those little things taken away from him far too soon.

The only way to stop his mind from drifting was to keep busy. So gardening was a great way of doing that.

The doorbell rang with the classic ding dong ring. It rang several times before Lewis heard it. He ran down the stairs, jumping every other stair as he always does.

Even in the daytime Lewis was cautious and looked through the spy hole, that he could only just manage to see through.

It was Sally, so he opened the door.

Sally is standing all smiles in her pretty purple dress and brown shoes with tiny heels that only Sally could get away with. The first thing he noticed about Sally when he opened the door was the strong smell of perfume. It almost made Lewis cough it was so strong. She was holding a bouquet of different coloured flowers.

Lewis politely smiled. Whenever he saw Sally, he always remembered hearing his mum telling Carlos that she was secretly in love with him.

"Hello, Lewis! How are you?"

Lewis replies abruptly but politely as possible.

"I'm OK. Did you want to see Dad?"

"Yes, and you of course."

"Hang on I'll get Dad." Lewis runs off towards the sound of the lawn mower in the garden. A few seconds and the hum of the lawnmower stops and Lewis returns with Carlos.

"Hey."

Carlos also notices the smell of her perfume but smiles politely.

"Sally. Come on in."

Sally stretches her arm out holding the bouquet of flowers.

"I brought some flowers. I thought it might be nice to brighten the place up a bit."

Sally pushes in front of Carlos and makes her way into the living room as if she lived there. She stops in the middle of the room and makes a half turn.

"All we need now are some flower vases."

Carlos smiles.

"That's very thoughtful, Sally."

Carlos picks up a vase from the table, but Sally's expression said everything.

"No, that is far too small."

"Lewis, can you fetch two vases from the kitchen cupboard please."

"OK."

There is a slightly awkward silence until Lewis returns with two brightly coloured vases.

"Wow, how perfect they will look. Very bright aren't they?"

"Tanya bought them in the sale."

Sally gestures with her bouquet of flowers to Lewis.

"Pop them on the table and we can spread them between the two vases, can't we?"

Lewis turns his head to Carlos, away from Sally and rolls his eyes.

"Now if there is anything you need just let me know. I'm always about getting bits and pieces for my old ladies and gents as you know and Alice keeps me on my toes so one or two more bits won't hurt."

"There's nothing at the moment that I can think of."

Sally is almost finished arranging the flowers into the two vases. She steps back and throws her arms apart on either side of her.

"There. What do you think?"

"Well thank you, Sally! Is there no end to your talents?"

Sally smiles in a girly fashion.

"Oh thank you, Carlos."

She looks at Lewis whose face doesn't look very impressed but as soon as he sees Sally looking, he smiles.

"What do you think, Lewis? Do you like them?"

"Yes, great."

Sally turns to Carlos.

"Now, I have a free night tonight, and I can soon get a baby sitter. How about I bring some of my cooking over and then you two can just relax tonight and not worry about a thing?"

"That sounds wonderful but…"

Before Carlos could finish his sentence, Sally butts in.

"That's settled then, what time?"

"Sally, I'm really sorry! I really would prefer to have an evening alone with Lewis. I've had quite a time."

Lewis smirks then sits down in his favourite armchair and picks up his mobile phone and puts his earplugs in and listens to his music.

"Oh, yes I understand. I'm sorry. I should have thought about that. Me and my big old mouth."

"I hope you're not offended. I am grateful, thank you and thank you for the lovely flowers too."

Sally looks at Lewis to wave but he is busy with his eyes closed listening to his music.

"No problem! Well, let me leave you two alone and to get on with… well whatever you are going to do."

Carlos leads her to the front door.

Once they leave the room, Lewis takes his earphones out and sighs, then gives out a little giggle and listens to the rest of Carlos and Sally's conversation.

"Well, thank you for dropping by."

"That's no problem, now if you need anything. Anything."

"Yes anything."

"Yes, OK."

Carlos watches until she has left the garden then closes the door. He puts his back against the door, closes his eyes and sighs with relief.

When Carlos opens his eyes, Lewis is standing watching with his arms crossed. He mimics her.

"If you need anything. Anything."

Carlos smiles and then laughs.

"She so wants you, Dad."

Chapter Twenty-Six

As the night sky twinkled with tiny stars and the shadows loomed across the graveyard at St John's Church. A low mist swirled around the stones, monuments and tombs reflected and lit by the full moon. The church ticked over to 1:10 am. Mist began to seep from under the crypt door and slowly climb up the church wall.

***

The lights in Sally's house were all tuned out except a small orange night light on the landing, which Sally likes to keep on in case, Alice, her seven year old daughter needs to go to the toilet.

Sally tosses and turns in her sleep hearing giggling while she sleeps. She suddenly wakes up and sits bolt upright in bed, sweating. There is silence. She moans to herself.

"Another damn nightmare."

Then she hears the giggling again. She stops moving in her bed, sitting very still and listens. There is silence.

Sally lies back down and closes her eyes. As she starts to drift off into the land of dreams she hears laughing.

Sally opens her eyes and listens for a second, there is definitely laughing. She sits up and switches the bed sidelight on, then checks her mobile phone for the time.

It is 1:45 am. She sighs.

"Alice."

Sally throws back the quilt cover and swings her legs out of the bed. Then finds her slippers with her toes and she slips them on.

She stands up wearing a skimpy silk night dress, then collects her matching silk dressing gown from the back of her dressing table chair and slips it on.

Still half asleep, she leaves the bedroom.

Once on the landing, she switches the landing light on and squints at the brightness of the light. She opens Alice's door just enough to peak her head in.

Alice is fast asleep.

Sally whispers to Alice, just in case she is pretending.

"Alice, are you asleep?"

There is no movement at all.

Sally leaves the door ajar which leaves a shard of light slicing across Alice's bedroom.

Sally switches of the light, leaving Alice's room in darkness, apart from the moon that is lighting up the room. Sally drapes her dressing gown back over the chair at her dressing table and gets back into bed then turns off her bedside light and snuggles down.

Alison is asleep and the moonlight is just catching her fair cheeks and golden hair.

A figure steps out of the dark shadow in the corner of the room. It is Pipa. Her eyes burning red staring at Alison lying in her bed. Her sharp teeth showing as she begins to smile.

Chapter Twenty-Seven

Carlos is already in the driving seat of his jeep when Lewis jumps in and slams the door. Carlos doesn't look too impressed.

"There is no need to slam the door, Lewis."

Lewis shrugs his shoulders and thinks for a second.

"Well, I don't know why we have to go so early."

Carlos fastens his seat belt.

"Well, I have a few errands to do and you can keep me company."

"Yes Dad, but really? This early?"

"Well the truth is, I couldn't sleep, so I thought, breakfast out at the cafe. My treat and then onto the library and then get a few bits at the corner shop."

Lewis fastens his belt as Carlos turns on the engine.

"OK."

"Breakfast out sounds good, right?"

"Yes, I suppose so."

Lewis smiles.

As Carlos reverses out of the drive onto the road, he smiles back at Lewis. He switches the indicators on. And as he pulls away, he turns the music, on driving off down the road.

"There's nothing like a bit of country music to brighten the day."

"Yeah, if you like sad songs."

"Hey, they're not all sad, they are fun. You need to hear…"

Carlos turns the music up.

"Now this is a great tune, you have to agree."

"Yeah OK Dad, I get the message."

Carlos laughs.

"Anyway, the books could have waited."

"They are already overdue. I have to pay a fine as it is for them"

"Well, Mrs Brown will only want to know your business. You know what she's like, Mum always hated going in there."

"Well, I will be as quick as I can so she won't have a chance."

"She will."

Carlos pulls up outside the library and Lewis jumps out. He runs in with his bag of books.

Chapter Twenty-Eight

Sally puts a packet of cereal on the kitchen table and opens the kitchen door and calls up the stairs to Alice.

"Alice, breakfast."

Sally continues to clear up the kitchen and unload the dishwasher. Sally looks up at the big red clock on the wall it is 8:45 am. She huffs and shouts out into the hall and up the stairs again.

"Alice?"

Sally pauses and listens at the door to see if she can hear Alice moving about. She calls again.

"Alice. Are you coming?"

Sally mumbles under her breath as she finishes emptying the dishwasher.

What is she playing at; she's always up by now.

Sally opens up the cupboard and places her bright green plates next to her purple cereal bowels; nothing matches in Sally's kitchen.

Just like her clothes her decor matches her dress sense! And not a lot of it!

Even the cups and saucers are different colours, the walls are painted sunshine yellow, the kitchen cupboards are bright red with silver handles, the range cooker is in green, and the list goes on and on including the sponges.

The only thing of ordinary white is the tea towels.

The door opens slowly and Alice walks in rubbing her eyes. Sally turns and sees her.

"Hello darling! I thought you had fallen down the hole!"

Alice yawns.

"I'm so tired."

Alice sits down at the table and looks down at her big empty purple cereal bowl.

Sally looks at the table then at Alice.

"Where's your glass?"

"Oh, I forgot it. Its upstairs by the bed, I'll go and get it."

"No, don't worry. I'll get it, I'm quicker than you."

Sally rushes through the door and up the stairs into Alice's room. She rubs her arms as the room is cold. She then notices that the curtains are blowing slightly, as the breeze comes through the open window. Sally closes the window and grabs the glass from the bedside table and runs back down the stairs, through the hallway and back into the kitchen.

She puts the glass into the empty dishwasher and takes a big breath looking at Alice, sitting at the table with her eyes shut.

"Wakey wakey!"

Alice opens her eyes.

"I was just resting them."

"Well you've had all night to do that. Right! Let's get you some breakfast. You can have rice Krispies or cornflakes?"

Alice looks up with her big blue eyes which she inherited from Sally.

"Rice Krispies, please Mummy!"

"OK, Rice Krispies it is then."

Sally empties the Rice Krispies into Alice's bowl and then pours the milk.

"Oh Alice, please don't open the window in your bedroom. It let's all the heat out of the room and all the insects get in. It was freezing when I went up there to collect your glass. I don't know how you can sleep with it so cold."

"OK Mummy, but I didn't."

"Well I didn't, and if you didn't, it must have been the boogie man."

"It wasn't all my fault Mummy, Pipa said to open it."

Sally dropped the bag of sugar onto the side from the cupboard. Luckily the bag was new so nothing spilt out. Sally turned and looked at Alice.

"Pipa? But Pipa …"

Sally nearly said Pipa was dead but she hadn't told Alice about Pipa yet so she stopped speaking about it quickly.

"Alison, you know that's not true. You don't need to make up stories to me darling."

Alice looked a little upset that Sally didn't believe her.

"I'm not, Mummy, honest."

Chapter Twenty-Nine

Carlos parks up in the street opposite Mrs Brown's convenience store. Lewis jump out onto the pavement while Carlos locks up the jeep.

They cross over the fairly quiet road and enter into the store. The little bell rings as the door opens and Mrs Brown opens her eyes and gets up from her chair.

Mrs Brown immediately smiles as Lewis and then Carlos walk towards the counter.

"Mrs Brown. Good morning."

"Good morning to you too and how are you Lewis? Oh you get more handsome with every day."

She looks up at Carlos.

"You are every inch your father."

She looks up at Carlos smiling which breaks into a yawn.

"Don't you agree?"

Lewis smiles as Carlos ruffles his dark hair.

"Sure is, Mrs Brown."

Mrs Brown yawns again.

"Are we keeping you up?"

Lewis giggles and Carlos laughs and then Mrs Brown joins in.

"I didn't get much sleep last night. I had a funny old night."

"Tell me about it. We've had a few of them, haven't we son?"

Lewis just agrees with a nod of his head.

"Do you know I woke up around 1:30 am and I could have sworn I saw young Susan Moorcroft standing at the foot of my bed."

Carlos looked straight at Lewis then back at Mrs Brown.

"She looked different. She looked evil, her eyes were all bloodshot."

Lewis pipes up trying to make light of the situation.

"Sound like a nightmare."

"She then just turned to smoke and disappeared, it was really horrible."

"That sounds like a proper nightmare, Mrs Brown."

"Yes, that's the worst nightmare I've ever had. That much I can tell you. I couldn't sleep after that, I sat up all night drinking coffee. It shook me up so much."

Carlos nods his head.

"I bet it did."

"Anyway, what can I help you with?"

"Oh, I only want a few bits; eggs, bread, butter, that sort of stuff."

Mrs Brown puts her hands on her hips.

"Well, I'll let you go off and do your shopping. I'll be sat here trying to get some shut eye."

Lewis smiles and jokes.

"We'll wake you when were done."

Mrs Brown sits back down on her chair and closes her eyes.

Lewis whispers to his dad.

"It's happening, Dad."

"I know."

"We have to get to the church and let Peter know."

Carlos reassures Lewis with a pat on the back.

"We will as soon as I have finished up here. I'll call him."

Carlos puts the last item into his basket. They wander over to the counter through the stacked up aisles of countless food products. Carlos then places the basket on the counter as quietly as possible. Lewis speaks to Mrs Brown.

"Hello, we are all done."

Mrs Brown opens her eyes and smiles.

"Are we all done then? Lovely! Right let us get this lot packed up for you."

Chapter Thirty

Sally always kept the curtain a little open just a few inches apart in the middle, just so that when she lay in bed she could watch the moon.

It always fascinated her; how it glows so bright amongst the tiny planets surrounding it. Just through that gap in the curtain it always gives just enough light to send a beam of light across her bed.

Sally lay asleep. She tossed and turned in her sleep and as the moonlight hit her face, it showed off the sweat on her forehead.

Laughing could be heard from Alice's room again but Sally slept through in her unsettled sleep.

Alice lay on her bed and Pipa stood beside her looking down smiling. Alice looking up at Pipa's pale face.

"I don't want to play anymore."

Pipa tilts her head to one side.

"But why?"

"I want to go to sleep now. Mummy will be cross if I'm tired again."

"I thought we were friends."

"We are; I just want to sleep."

"OK, I understand. Let me kiss you goodnight, like last night."

Alice turns her head to one side and pulls her hair away from her neck revealing two puncture marks on her neck.

"Close your eyes."

Alice closes her eyes shutting them tight. As Pipa stares at Alice her eyes turn blood red, she snarls as she rises into the air hovering above the bed, then suddenly she lunges and sinks her fangs into Alice's throat biting deep into the pale flesh and draining the blood and life from her.

Alice's tiny hands squeeze the covers tight. As her body's life slowly drained her tiny hands relaxed.

Pipa stood beside the bed looking at Alice, the blood still dripping from her mouth.

Alice's body twitched all over, then her eyes opened staring up at the ceiling. Pipa smiles and opened the bedroom window wide.

"Come, Alice."

Chapter Thirty-One

The kettle boils and Carlos pours the water into two mugs. The coffee granules swirl around the mug until they dissolve. Carlos calls out.

"Lewis, your tea is done."

Lewis calls down the stairs.

"OK."

Carlos finishes making the drinks and takes a packet of digestive biscuits from the cupboard and opens them while he sits down at the kitchen table.

He opens the newspaper and begins to read.

Lewis comes in, still in his pyjama bottoms. Carlos speaks with a mouth full of biscuit.

"You need to put your sugar in, I forgot."

Lewis takes two spoons full of sugar and puts them in his tea and stirs it while he sits down.

"What's in the news?"

Carlos looks up at Lewis.

"Nothing much so far."

Carlos notices that he still has his pyjama bottoms on and its almost midday.

"Lewis, why are you still in your pyjamas?"

"I was doing stuff."

"On that computer? It's nearly 12:00 pm and you're not even dressed."

"OK Dad, I'll just drink this and then I'll get dressed."

Carlos shakes his head.

"OK."

The doorbell rings and Carlos looks up from his newspaper and Lewis looks up from blowing his mug of tea. Carlos puts his newspaper down.

"Now who can that be?"

Carlos gets up and opens the kitchen door and listens with his head in the hall. The doorbell rings again so Carlos enters the hall and opens the front door.

Sally stood in front of Carlos looking quite rough. Her hair looked a mess and she had little to no makeup on at all, which was very unusual as Sally liked to wear bold colours to match her dress sense.

"Sally!"

Sally smiled.

"Just calling to see how you both are"

"We are fine. Do you want to come in?"

Carlos knew something was wrong. Sally wasn't her cheery self, full of energy and always happy, today she was deflated and sad and looking a mess.

"Go into the kitchen, Lewis is in there."

Sally entered the kitchen while Carlos closed the front door and followed in after her.

"Can I get you a drink? Tea? Coffee?"

Sally nods.

"Tea please."

Sally sits down. Lewis stares at her then at Carlos then back at Sally. Lewis thought she looked like she was in another world, in a world of her own. Sally looks up at Lewis and tries to smile.

"Hi, Lewis."

Lewis felt a little uneasy.

"Hi, Sally."

Carlos put a mug of tea in front of her and the bowl of sugar.

"The kettle had only just boiled. Here!"

Sally looked down at the tea.

"Thanks."

"How are you?"

Sally bursts into tears.

"What's up? What's the matter?"

"Alice."

Sally is sobbing and the tears are rolling down her face.

"I didn't know who to go to, she's gone."

Carlos looks at Lewis.

"Gone?"

Sally just nods still crying.

Carlos gets up and grabs the box of unopened tissues from the side. He opens the box and gives them to Sally.

"What do you mean gone?"

"I don't know. I got up this morning and went into her room and she had gone."

"Have you checked the doors?"

Sally nods wiping her nose.

"My baby, my little girl, where is she? I just don't understand where she could have gone. All the doors were locked."

Carlos stretches his hand out and holds her hand.

"I understand."

Sally snaps back at Carlos and Lewis looks a little shocked.

"You don't, no one can. Everything was shut, locked and she disappeared, only her bedroom window…"

Carlos cuts in.

"Her window was open?"

"Yes, she insisted it was to be kept open, for fresh air. And Pipa. Oh, it is all a mess I don't understand."

Lewis looks at Sally.

"Pipa?"

Carlos looks at Lewis then back at Sally.

"What about Pipa?"

Sally wipes her eyes and blows her nose.

"She said she played with her the night before she disappeared, she's only a child they have such imaginations. She was her best friend at school. She doesn't even know she is dead."

Carlos gets up while Sally composes herself after continuous crying. He opens a bottom cupboard and takes out vodka and some tonic then a glass from a wall cupboard. He begins to pour.

"Here, drink this. I think you need it."

"Thank you."

Sally sips it and coughs.

"It's strong."

"Yes, well my measurements are a bit way out I guess."

Carlos chuckles, trying to lighten the atmosphere.

"Tanya always liked a cheeky vodka."

Lewis looks up and smiles remembering his mum leaning against the sink drinking a vodka saying, "Don't tell your dad I've had a cheeky one, will you," knowing full well he would.

Sally smiles and finishes her Vodka. She lets out a large and rather loud sigh.

"I've taken up too much of your time. I'm sorry I should contact the police again to see if they have any updates."

"That sounds like a good idea. Well if you need us, we are here. OK?"

"Yes, thank you."

Sally enters the hall followed by Carlos. She opens the door, then as she steps outside she turns to Carlos and smiles.

"I could always pop back later if you like. I could make us all something to eat."

Carlos explains but feeling quite awkward knowing Sally's situation.

"That sounds lovely, but it's a bit difficult as I'm going to be at the church tonight with the vicar."

"Oh, the church? What's happened?"

Carlos had to think on his feet quickly.

The last thing he wanted was for Sally to impose on tonight's events as it will be hard enough to evaluate the situation without Sally finding out what they were really doing at the church.

"Oh yes. Nothing really just sorting out some last bits and pieces. Donations, that sort of thing."

Sally looked a little disappointed but Carlos had no option but to put her off.

"Well OK. Bye."

Carlos closes the door and rests his head against it for a sec while he thinks. Lewis enters and looks at his dad clearly unsettled by everything.

"She means well, Dad."

"Yes, I know."

They both move back into the kitchen and plonk themselves in their chairs.

"Nice excuse though, Dad."

Lewis giggles.

"Yes, I thought so. I could have said," Carlos puts on his best English accent, "sorry old gal we are off tonight to kill a few vampires."

Lewis and Carlos both giggle.

"She's so dizzy she would have said great idea, I will see you when you finish."

"No, she would have wanted to come."

Lewis finishes the rest of his tea then looks at Carlos looking out of the window at the sun shining in the garden.

"She still fancies you, Dad. Mum was right, she does, it's so obvious. That's why Mum didn't like her much."

"She did like her. Mum was just jealous of all women I came in close contact with."

Lewis thinks for a bit.

"Dad?"

Carlos looks at Lewis thinking he can almost see the cogs turning in his head.

"Yes?"

"I've been thinking about this holy water."

"Oh yes, what about it?"

"Well, all the vampires sleep in the crypt, don't they? And how deep would you say the crypt is?"

"I don't know without looking. I've never been in one before."

"Then maybe we should take a look while it is daylight."

Chapter Thirty-Two

Peter is lighting the last of the candles in the church as Lewis and Carlos stroll in. Lewis calls out to Peter creating an echo that resounds all around the walls of St John's Church.

"Peter!"

Peter turns around and notices them walking up the aisle.

"Ah, Carlos, Lewis, I was wondering where you were? It's getting a bit late."

"Yes, the time goes by so fast."

"Yes, it does."

Carlos held up his mobile phone.

"I tried calling you this afternoon."

"I'm sorry I've been out most of the day and left my mobile phone at the vicarage."

"We've had quite a day haven't we, son?"

"Yes."

Lewis nods and continues to explain.

"It's Alice, she has gone missing."

Peter looks confused and thinks for second.

"Alice?"

Carlos explains.

"Sally's daughter, she's only seven. Sally came to the house today in a bad way. She said Pipa was playing with her daughter the night before."

Peter looks worried.

"But Pipa is dead."

Carlos agrees.

"Yes, I know. This is what Alice told Sally the day before she disappeared. She said she was playing with her in the night."

Peter shakes his head.

"I'm a little confused, so you think Pipa has taken Alice?"

"Yes. Well, that's what we think. We haven't told Sally that. We didn't want to give anything away. She would probably think we were mad. However, she did say that she found the window wide open in her bedroom and all the doors were still locked."

Peter rubs his chin.

"Oh dear, this really is getting worse, isn't it?"

Carlos and Lewis both agree. Peter quickly brushes by Carlos and Lewis.

"Come on. We mustn't waste anymore time. It's getting dark."

Lewis looks up at Carlos.

"What about the policemen?"

Peter stops as he hears Lewis's question.

"Well the constable cannot make it this evening, he has some problem at the station. He said he would meet us here midday tomorrow."

They all continue walking out of the church into the churchyard. Carlos huffs.

"Well, that's another night those things will be out there."

Lewis looks up at Peter and Carlos.

"We will just have to be careful, that's all."

Carlos looked at Peter smiling, thinking how Lewis has grown up so fast and has started thinking like an adult and sometimes more rationally than himself.

"So, Lewis? Have you come up with anything?"

Lewis stops to speak.

"Yes, I have. But first we need to see how big the crypt is. Well, Dad does."

Carlos turns to Peter.

"Yep, that's my job."

Peter looks nervous.

"The crypt?"

Lewis continues.

"Yes. We need to know how deep the crypt is and how big it is unless you know the measurements."

"Oh I don't know. It's not that small. But may I ask why?"

"Lewis has an idea about the holy water."

"Oh?"

Lewis asks very seriously.

"How much water can you bless in one go to make it holy."

"I once blessed a stream."

Peter looks up at the sky, it was getting darker.

"Funnily, it's the stream that runs around the whole village. Come on we better get a move on its getting dark."

Lewis smiles and looks at Carlos.

"That's excellent. They won't be able to pass the stream, it will prevent them from spreading outside of the village. Well unless they turn into bats."

Peter looks horrified at the thought of these vampires spreading any further than they have already. It could open up a can of worms.

"Don't worry, Peter. I think the village population is enough to keep them here for a while."

"I hope you're right, Carlos."

"We will need to flood the crypt with holy water."

"Well, how do you suppose we do that?"

"Well, you know I work for the water company. We use those huge lorries containing water. Maybe you could bless the water in one of those?"

"Flush the bastards out!"

Peter and Carlos both look at Lewis smiling cheekily.

"That's what you said, Dad."

"Yes, well."

Peter laughs.

"It's OK."

"I suppose I could. But would people ask questions?"

Lewis interjects.

"Not if Constable Connor authorised it."

Peter agrees shrugging his shoulders.

"Well its worth a try, isn't it?"

"It's all we have to go with at the moment. Now I need to see inside the crypt."

Peter looks around as the churchyard is getting darker.

"It's getting really dark now. Do you think it's wise?"

"I only want to have a quick glance just to see roughly how much water we are going to need. Also I need to know how long a hose we need. I'll be in and out in a flash."

Chapter Thirty-Three

The evening is drawing in and the churchyard at St John's is mostly in shadow as the sun goes down.

Peter is starting to panic as he looks around fumbling with the large bunch of keys.

Eventually finding the correct key, he inserts it into the rust keyhole of the crypt door and unlocks it.

The door creaks as it opens up into darkness. There is silence as they all stop to listen.

Peter puts his hand into his pocket and pulls out a small torch and gives it to Carlos.

"Here is a torch, you will need it. It's not the best, I only use it for finding the keyholes in the dark. Be careful! There isn't much light down there."

Carlos and Lewis enter the crypt and slowly walk down the cold stone stairs. The torch lighting up very little as they head down into the darkness of the crypt. There is a strange smell like old blood from a butcher's counter and the air is thin and musty. The dust is picked out in the beam from the torch and very little light came in from the broken narrow window.

Peter was leaning against the crypt door staring down the stairs into darkness waiting for Carlos and Lewis to rush back out.

Instead, he felt a hand on his shoulder which made him jump out of his skin.

Peter turned to see Sally smiling at him.

"My goodness, you nearly frightened me to death."

"Oh sorry, Peter. I thought I might find Carlos here, he said he would be here."

"Well yes, he's down in the crypt…"

Sally excitedly interrupts.

"Oh a crypt! I will go down. I've never been in one."

Sally rushes past Peter and through the door without a second thought.

Peter tries to stop her.

"Sally no please…"

But it was too late, she disappeared in a second. As she gets a few steps down, she slips on the worn out damaged step, screaming out as she falls to the bottom, landing on the floor, bashing her head on a corner stone.

Carlos and Lewis jump and immediately turn around and shine the torch in the direction of the noise.

Sally is lying at the bottom of the stairs, her head is cut quite badly and blood is running down her face from the open wound. Not even thinking about Sally's injuries, Carlos whispers to Sally.

"What are you doing here?"

Carlos and Lewis move as quickly as they can in the dark to get to Sally, but before they reach her a vampire pounces out from the shadows and grabs hold of her.

The beam of light from Carlos's torch catches the vampire sinking her teeth into Sally's throat while lifting her up off of the ground a good few inches.

Sally's body is shaking all over as if she was being electrocuted. Her body like a charged mess of nerves.

The blood is running from the mouth of the vampire as she snarls and stares at Carlos and Lewis. Her eyes are blood red and staring, seemingly to enjoy seeing them both looking terrified.

She opens her mouth and releases Sally from her grip. Sally drops to the floor as the vampire lowers to the ground.

In a split second the vampire reaches out and grabs hold of Lewis's arm.

Lewis screams out.

"Dad, my arm."

Carlos quickly shines a torch on the floor and finds an old candlestick covered on dust and cobwebs. In a fit of rage he grabs the candlestick and swings it round with all his might and smashes the vampire in the face. The vampire immediately lets go of Lewis. Carlos screams out.

"Run."

Carlos is practically pushing Lewis up the stairs, checking behind him every second.

Lewis is out of breath but still manages to speak.

"What about Sally?"

Carlos and Lewis almost reach the top of the stairs.

"Keep running. Just get out."

Lewis runs out of the crypt door first followed immediately by a very frantic Carlos.

"Lock the door, Peter. Lock the door, quickly."

Peter looks very nervous pulling the crypt door shut he remembers Sally.

"What about Sally?"

Carlos shouts at Peter.

"They've got her. Lock the door."

Peter slams the door shut and fumbles for his keys praying under his breath.

While Lewis is bent over still getting his breath back after the running and the shock, Carlos continues to explain what happened.

"She fell and cut her head, they grabbed her. They almost got Lewis."

Peter finds the correct key and locks the door.

Peter takes hold of Carlos's arm.

"We should leave now."

Lewis notices mist starting to seep from under the crypt door.

"Look, Peter. The mist."

Peter looks at Lewis and Carlos with panic in his eyes.

"Quick, let's go."

Lewis stops Peter.

"Do you have some holy water with you?"

"Yes, in my pocket."

Peter fumbles and finds the bottle his hands are shaking.

"Quickly, throw it on the mist."

Peter's hands tremble as he opens the bottle of holy water. He quickly pours the water across the mist seeping under the door. The mist immediately retracts back under the door and into the crypt. A loud hiss can be heard behind the door. Carlos grabs peter and Lewis by their arms.

"Run."

Peter looks at Carlos in sheer panic.

"Where?"

"Anywhere! Your home, the vicarage, it's nearer."

Chapter Thirty-Four

Tanya's blood red eyes appear from the shadows as she walks into the shard of moonlight beaming through the window. When she notices Sally lying on the floor, she snarls.

Sally's eyes flutter as she regains consciousness and her eyes at first are blurred. When her eyes regain vision and adjust to the darkness, she recognises Tanya standing in front of her.

"Tanya?"

Tanya snarls again as she grabs Sally and throws her across the crypt like a rag doll. Sally screams as she plunges into a dusty tomb.

The force of Sally hitting the tomb causes the dust to move into the air and the cobwebs to swing in the breeze.

Tanya slowly walks through the shadows towards Sally.

"Yes."

Sally pleads with Tanya.

"Please."

Tanya smiles at Sally, revealing her sharp fangs.

"Please?"

Sally begins to cry.

"Let me go, please! Let me go."

The tears roll down Sally's face as she continues to sob.

Tanya tilts her head staring and grinning at Sally, watching her squirm with fright.

"You will join us."

From every corner of the crypt and from every shadow vampires close in on Sally.

Sally notices the vampires and begins to shake from head to foot in panic.

"No please, let me go! I'll help you, please?"

There are echoes of giggling that fill the tomb.

"Help? Yes, you will. You will become one of us, you will breed."

Sally wipes her eyes with her hand.

"Breed?"

Tanya laughs out loud and the other vampires join in. Sally tries to move but her leg is injured and she yelps in pain.

"Breed? I don't understand. You want …"

Tanya cuts in.

"It's the only way we can survive."

Sally shakes her head.

"No, I won't do it."

Tanya's voice changes, she tilts her head back opening her mouth gasping, revealing her sharp fangs. She then looks down and stares at Sally leaning forward.

"You have already been bitten."

Sally feels her neck with her fingers and remembers. Tanya smiles.

"You don't get a choice."

Tanya stands upright, her eyes glow red as she snarls, and she then tilts her head back and hisses.

Several vampires move in from the shadows and surround her. Tanya rips open the front of Sally's dress revealing her large firm breasts. She cups her hand around her breast and sinks her fangs deep into her flesh. Sally screams as the blood pours from her breast.

The other vampires are waiting patiently for their turn, standing naked and staring with their blood red eyes and pale flesh. As Tanya tilts her head back, the blood runs out from her mouth and down her neck.

Sally screaming in fright as Tanya lifts her arm up high and commands.

"Feed."

The vampires close in on Sally and start to bite her wrists and neck and breasts.

Sally is just lying there helpless, on the floor, as her blood and life is being drained from her. Sally's head falls to the side as her eyes roll to the back of her head, as Tanya continues to drink the blood from Sally's breast while two other vampires drink from her wrists.

Chapter Thirty-Five

Peter ushers Carlos and Lewis inside the vicarage as fast as he can and shuts the door and locks it. He turns to Carlos and Lewis.

"Go on through, make yourself comfortable. I'll follow you in a second. I just need to do something."

Carlos and Lewis do not hesitate as they make their way down the hall and enter the living room.

Leaving Peter to get on with whatever he planned to do.

Peter takes out another bottle of holy water and kisses it and then unscrews the cap and pours the water along the bottom of the door. He places the cap back on the bottle and makes his way down the hall and enters the living room only to find Carlos and Lewis sat down looking exhausted.

"Well, Carlos. I know what you need."

"Well, yes that too but I was thinking more like a drink."

"Now you are talking my language."

Peter looks in the cupboard.

"Mmm."

Carlos and Lewis watch patiently.

"Only wine, I'm afraid the brandy has gone. We managed to polish that off the last time. I shall have to get some more."

Peter pulls out a bottle of red from the wine rack.

"Wine is good."

"OK."

Peter looks at Lewis watching.

"And for you, young man? A mug of tea?"

"Yeah, that's sounds good, thank you."

Peter switches on the kettle and collects two glasses from the cupboard. Hanging the wine glasses between his fingers in one hand and the bottle of red in the other he places them down carefully onto the coffee table.

Carlos noticed a corkscrew already lying on the table with a couple of used corks lying loose on the table. One was still screwed to the end, so Carlos removed it and place it next to the others.

Peter clearly liked a glass of wine in the evening or maybe the occasional bottle.

The kettle boiled and Peter swiftly made Lewis his mug of tea, that he so very much needed after his ordeal.

Peter sat in his usual comfy office chair and watched Carlos pour the wine. As Carlos hands Peter the wine, Peter continued to talk.

"We need to work fast. I have poured holy water at the bottom of the vicarage door. I just need to be sure."

"OK."

Lewis sips his tea then tells Peter.

"We need to flood the crypt tomorrow evening."

"But first, I have to prepare."

Lewis shuffles in his seat making himself more comfortable then asks.

"It's just a prayer, isn't it?"

"Yes it is, but I have to bless the salt first."

Lewis tilts his head and questions Peter. Lewis is a very inquisitive boy and Peter loves to see such enthusiasm in people especially children.

"Salt?"

Peter explains. Even Carlos is intrigued.

"Yes. You have to bless the salt."

"Why?"

Peter continues to explain.

"Holy water is a mixture of salt and water. Both the water and salt are blessed."

Carlos props himself up and leans forward.

"How long will it take?"

"Maybe thirty minutes or so."

Carlos leans back in his chair and continues to sip his wine.

"OK Peter, in the morning, I will pick you up."

Peter puts his glass down onto his desk.

"Stay here tonight I have room for you both. Besides I could do with the company."

Carlos could tell Peter was a bag of nerves so he agreed.

"To be honest, I think we all can."

Peter smiles and holds up his glass.

"I'll drink to that."

Carlos and Lewis both hold their glass and mug up too.

Chapter Thirty-Six

Constable Connor, Peter, Carlos and Lewis are admiring Carlos's six-wheel water tanker. Carlos's foreman, a tall black man with a strong accent, walks over.

"You should be OK over here, you won't be disturbed."

Peter smiles and Carlos pats him on the back.

"Thanks, buddy."

"If you need anything else I'm sure Carlos can help. I will be in my office."

Peter questions Carlos.

"Did you put the salt in?"

Carlos nods.

"Yes, I did."

Constable Connor looks confused?

"Salt?"

Peter explains briefly.

"The salt makes up the holy water."

"Oh, that's interesting, I didn't know that."

Peter takes out the bible as the water tank begins to fill. Constable Connor whispers to Carlos. "How long does it take to fill up? This tank is huge."

"Well, I would say no more than about thirty minutes. We have it being pumped in. It works pretty much the same as a pool pump only a little faster."

Constable Connor nods his head.

"Interesting."

Peter crosses himself, then the air and begins the blessing reading from the Bible.

"I exorcise thee in the name of God the Father almighty, and in the name of Jesus Christ His Son, our Lord, and in the power of the Holy Ghost, that you may be able to put to flight all the power of the enemy, and be able to root out and supplant that enemy and his apostate angels; through the power of our Lord Jesus Christ, who will come to judge the living and the dead and the world by fire. God, who for the salvation of the human race has built your greatest mysteries upon this substance, in your kindness hear our prayers and pour down the power of your blessing into this element, prepared by many purifications. May this your creation be a vessel of divine grace to dispel demons and sicknesses, so that everything that it is sprinkled on in the homes and buildings of the faithful will be rid of all unclean and harmful things. Let no pestilent spirit, no corrupting atmosphere, remain in those places: may all the schemes of the hidden enemy be dispelled. Let whatever might trouble the safety and peace of those who live here be put to flight by this water, so that health, gotten by calling Your Holy Name, may be made secure against all attacks. Through Our Lord Jesus Christ, Thy Son, Who liveth and reigneth with Thee in the unity of the Holy Ghost, God, world without end. Amen."

Constable Connor chats quietly with Carlos as Peter finishes up.

"Are you sure this will work? If it doesn't, I'm gonna have egg on my face. People have been asking a lot of questions."

"If this doesn't work, you will have more than egg on your face to worry about."

Peter walks over to Carlos and Constable Connor with Lewis.

"So, are we all done here then?"

Peter puts his hands up.

"I am."

"Great, then I think we should get some rest now if we can."

Carlos and Peter agree.

"I agree. I will see you all at the church tonight. I will be waiting."

Carlos shakes Peter's hand.

"Thank you, Peter."

"No problem. Go and get some rest."

"I have a feeling I am going to need it."

Carlos and Lewis walk over to the jeep and they both jump in and drive off. Carlos toots his horn as they drive away.

Constable Connor and Peter wave.

"Come on, Peter. Let me get you back to St John's; you need to get some rest too."

"Yes, I think I do and so must you."

"I'll try. Come on."

They head over to Constable Connor's police car and within minutes they drive away in the direction of the church.

***

Peter waves to Constable Connor as he drives off. Peter takes a big sigh and enters St John's graveyard almost in a daze. Peter walks down the winding path when Larry moves out from behind a tree carrying his shovel over his shoulder.

Peter jumps and lets out a yelp.

"Good God."

"Oh I'm sorry, Peter. I didn't mean to make you jump."

"No, its OK. I'm just a little tired that's all."

Larry follows Peter as he walks along the path.

"I haven't seen much of you the last few days?"

"No, I've had a few problems to sort out."

"Oh."

Larry pauses then continues.

"I think you might have a few more."

Peter stops walking and stops to listen.

"Why?"

"I was coming to see you about it. Them chaps that was killed at the lighthouse."

Peter looks very concerned and at the same time he also looks worried.

"All their bodies have gone."

"Dear God."

Larry puts his hand on Peters shoulder.

"I don't think God had anything to do with it. Something's not quite right around here lately."

Peter hurries off, leaving Larry standing on his own wondering what is going on.

Chapter Thirty-Seven

Carlos is driving with Lewis to St John's church in the water tanker. Lewis is watching the road and the trees blowing gently in the breeze. There are very little lights and the road looks wet due to the damp air.

"It's so quiet."

"Sure is. What is it 8:30, a quarter to nine?"

Lewis checks the watch.

"Yeah! 8:37."

"See, not far out, we shouldn't be too long now. Another five minutes I guess."

"OK."

"Are you nervous?"

"Yeah, I think so."

Carlos smiles and slaps Lewis's leg.

"Don't be son. I got yaw back. We are gonna drown them bastards in their own shit. You'll see."

"Yeah, flush the bastards out."

Lewis laughs and Carlos joins in.

"Hey, that's my line."

They reach St John's Church and Peter is waiting for them by the gate. Carlos calls out through his open window.

"Hey."

Peter opens up the double gates so Carlos can drive up to the church.

"Where's your yard keeper?"

Peter looks up while opening the gate wide.

"Larry?"

"Yeah."

"Oh, he's about. I think he's at home. He'll be over later, normally locks up after 10:30–11:00ish. That's if he doesn't fall asleep."

Carlos smiles and continues to drive through the gates slowly and up to the church.

Carlos parks up the water truck and jumps out. Lewis jumps out and shuts his door.

Peter meets them at the crypt. Carlos rubs his hands and looks around the church yard, watching the mist swirling around the trees and bushes.

"Well, it's getting misty."

"Yes, it seems to be around this area more than around the town."

"Sure."

"I haven't told Larry about any of this. I think he would panic."

Walking towards the church through the mist, Constable Connor and Sergeant Pike appear. Peter waves.

Constable Connor looks at the water truck and then at Carlos.

"Well, what a big boy."

Carlos smiles and jokes.

"Well, thanks for saying. I've had no complaints."

Peter clears his throat.

"Sorry Peter."

"It's OK."

Carlos looks around at everybody.

"Well, we are all here. Shall we get started?"

Sergeant Pike looks at his watch. It's showing 9:05 pm.

Carlos runs to the truck and pulls the hosepipe out and runs up to the crypt door holding the nozzle. He drops it on the floor and puts his hands on his hips as he addresses everyone.

"We will need to go back down into the crypt."

Peter looks nervous and asks.

"Can't you do it from up here?"

Carlos shakes his head.

"No."

Peter continues and pleads.

"It's far too dangerous. What if something happens again?"

"It's a chance we have to take."

"But you will be risking your life. Look what happened to Sally."

Carlos shrugs his shoulders. He seems to have got some inner strength from somewhere and his mind was set for work.

"Someone has to go down. It is to make sure there are no folds in the hose pipe."

Constable Connor thinks for a second.

"Did you say, Sally?"

Peter turns to the Constable and nods his head agreeing.

"Yes, I'm afraid so, Last evening, it's a long story."

Lewis interjects.

"I almost got bit too."

Carlos watches them chatting.

"Come on guys. I need some help, we need to work fast. We need to make sure there are no folds in the pipe."

Constable Connor looks over to Pike.

"Pike will go down."

Sergeant Pike looks at Constable Connor in shock.

"Thanks, constable. Why can't you go?"

"Because I'm a constable! And you're not. And also because I said so!"

Carlos tries the crypts door and it is still locked.

"Can we open this door?"

Peter fumbles in his pocket as he walks over to the door and pulls out a bunch of keys. He looks at Carlos then unlocks the door.

Carlos opens the door wide it is dark and the smell of blood wafts up the stairwell and out through the door.

Pike waves his hand in front of his face looking at Constable Connor.

"It's stinks."

Carlos carries on.

"Right, this is the plan. Pike will go down, I will follow making sure there are no folds in the pipe. As soon as that is done, we get out of there as quick as possible."

Constable Connor looks at Pike.

"You got that, Pike?"

Sergeant Pike nods.

"Yes, constable."

Carlos continues.

"And sergeant, be careful of the stairs, they are not too clever and it is dark. I will shine the torch as best I can."

Sergeant Pike agrees and looks down the dark stairwell then looks back at Carlos.

"Constable, can I put you in charge of the water valve?"

Constable Connor nods in agreement.

"Of course."

"It's pretty simple, you just turn it anti-clockwise to open the valve. Lewis, if you stand at the top of the stairs, I will signal you to open the valve. You then signal Constable Connor. OK?"

"OK, Dad."

Carlos looks at Peter.

"Is there anything I can do?"

Carlos smiles and puts his hand on Peters shoulder.

"You can pray for us down there."

Peter blows out air looking worried.

Carlos looks at Constable Connor straight in the eye.

"Constable, I'm putting my trust in you, that should there be any delays or anything, you just turn the water on full. Have you got that?"

Constable agrees.

"The water tap is on the side of the lorry. Lewis knows where it is."

Carlos looks at Pike.

"OK, are you ready?"

Sergeant Pike nods his head nervously; he glances at Constable Connor and Peter then Lewis. Carlos turns on the torch.

"OK, let go as quick as you can."

Carlos calls out, "Go."

As if it was the start of a race. And in some ways it was exactly that. A race against time.

Carlos puts the torch in his mouth as they run through the door. Sergeant Pike carefully makes his way down to the bottom of the stairs following the beam of light coming from Carlos's torch which he was aiming strategically with his mouth.

He finally reaches the bottom. Carlos follows closely behind checking the hose pipe as often as he can and making sure he doesn't trip up over it at the same time. Satisfied that the hose is placed correctly, Carlos whispers to Pike, "OK, let's get out. It's all OK."

They both turn to head up the stairs when all of a sudden out of the darkness, a vampire jumps from the ceiling and lands behind them. As she hisses at them they both turn to look. Carlos's torch flashes across the vampire's face. Pike yells out.

"Shit."

Carlos instantly recognises her to be Tanya.

Tanya hisses again at Carlos and Sergeant Pike, her eyes blazing red and her teeth sharp as razors.

The anger and frustration showing on her face. And the evil and menace, staring straight through them with her piercing red eyes. Carlos cannot stop trembling.

"Oh shit, Tanya."

Sergeant Pike is desperate to get up the stairs but Carlos stops dead in his tracks.

"Now what?"

Carlos looks around Sergeant Pike.

"I don't know."

Sergeant Pike gets hold of Carlos.

"Come on."

Carlos seems drawn in by Tanya.

"Tanya, it's me."

Tanya tilts her head on one side as if she is listening and begins to recognise Carlos. Some of the anger and rage leaves Tanya's face.

Sergeant Pike sees an opportunity to get up the stairs and as he attempts to run, another vampire grabs his leg from out of the shadow. Pike looks down and recognises it to be Susan Moorcroft. She snarls at Pike as he screams out for help.

"Carlos, get her off of me."

As Pike struggles to get free, he notices one of the large cocoons lying not too far from him. The light from Carlos's torch highlights the shine and the slimy texture. Pike struggle even more kicking the arms of Susan. She snarls and snaps at him, then she suddenly stops and turns her head as if she had sensed something happening behind her.

Pike could not believe his eyes when the cocoon started to split open revealing a body of a woman. A perfectly formed naked women. Her body dripping with slime, she breaks out pushing the soft ball shaped shell from around her. The slime drips from her naked body as she stands up. She stares at Pike while she wipes the slime from her breasts. Her eyes are blood red; she opens up her mouth revealing her long fangs. Pike in shock shouts out.

"What the fuck?"

Sally still holding on to Pikes ankle, watches the new born slowly walk over towards her, feeling her fangs with her tongue as she licks her lips.

Carlos realises what's happening and explains to Pike.

"They are breeding. That's how they are born."

Tanya smiles at Carlos, and he notices that her eyes are now that normal pretty blue. She had a sort of normality about her as if she was changing back to the old Tanya that Carlos knew and loved. Smiling, she spoke gently to Carlos.

"We need you, Carlos. We have to survive. We need to breed to survive. Come to us."

Carlos is getting weaker and is almost in tears as he listens to Tanya's voice.

"What about Lewis?"

Pike listens and watches in disbelief that Carlos is falling into their trap, being hypnotised and drawn in by her evil charm. Pike has had and seen enough and screams out at Carlos.

"She's a fucking vampire, Carlos, for fuck sake."

Tanya's suddenly turns her head to face Pike and smiles. Her eyes turn red and evil spreads across her pale face. Pike shouts at Tanya.

"Fuck you."

She turns her head back to Carlos, back to the sweet Tanya that Carlos loved. Tanya carries on speaking softly to Carlos.

"Lewis will come to us. He will have no choice."

Without warning Pike gets dragged away further into the crypt by Sally. Three more vampires climb down from the walls towards Pike. He screams out pleading to Carlos.

"Carlos, help me for god's sake."

Tanya laughs out loud her face seems to change back to that evil demonic vampire that she is. She bares her fangs.

Lewis hears Sergeant Pike scream out. He turns immediately to Peter.

"I think they are in trouble."

Lewis shouts down the stairs to Carlos.

"Dad?"

Constable Connor runs over to the crypt door.

"What's happening?"

Peter explains as quickly as he can.

"We don't know. Listen."

A scream is heard.

Lewis looks worried and calls after Carlos again.

"Dad."

There is no answer so Lewis attempts to run down the stairs. Constable Connor grabs hold of him before he can.

"No, Lewis. Let me turn the water on."

Constable Connor runs over to the truck while Peter and Lewis watch and listen.

More screams can be heard from the crypt. They both look at each other as Peter crosses himself. Peter notices that Constable Connor is struggling to open the water valve on the truck and calls over.

"Quickly, constable. Quickly."

Constable shouts across struggling to open the valve.

"It won't open. I can't get it to open."

Lewis runs over to Constable Connor and also tries to open it, it's either rusted stuck or he isn't strong enough either. Looking very worried, Lewis jumps up into the cabin of the truck and finds the tool bag. There is a big old wrench lying in the bag, so Lewis grabs it and jumps back down.

"Get out of the way."

Lewis take a big swing down on the water valve and old dirt and paint and rust all fall from around the valve releasing it. The valve moves.

"It's open."

Constable Connor pats Lewis on the back smiling.

"Out of my way, let me open the damn thing right up."

Lewis smiles and shouts over to Peter.

"It's open, Peter."

Looking at Constable Connor, Lewis continues.

"Let's flush the bastards out."

Constable Connor laughs.

Peter crosses himself again and continues to watch the door of the crypt.

Carlos is still trapped against a tomb by Tanya. She snarls as she opens her top revealing her breasts. Her face changes back to the Tanya that Carlos once loved.

"You still want me, don't you my love? We can be together for all eternity."

Pike feels the water touching his hands on the floor. He calls over to Carlos still fighting off the vampires.

"Carlos."

Carlos also notices the water heading his way. He continues to play along with Tanya hoping that she won't suspect anything.

Out of the corner of his eye he sees that the cocoon is starting to burn and melt as the holy water touches it.

Loud screams come from all around the crypt as the vampires come in contact with the water.

Sally releases Pike from her grip as her legs start to burn she screams out in agony.

"It's burning."

Pike quickly covers his body in the holy water rolling in it making sure his whole body is drenched.

Carlos tries to keep Tanya on his side pretending he is still in her trance.

"Tanya, I will get Lewis."

Tanya can see the water burning the vampires. She snarls in anger when she realises she is being trapped.

Carlos doesn't have any time to think. He quickly jumps up and grabs hold of the hosepipe and sprays Tanya in the face.

"Run, Pike run. You are protected. You are covered in holy water. Quick, let's get out."

Pike watches Carlos from the stairs as he quickly turns the pipe on himself covering himself in the holy water.

Tanya is frantic, her face still burning from the holy water standing on top a tomb watching the water rising around her. She screams and jumps at Carlos in rage but Carlos is too quick, he moves out of the way and Tanya lands on a broken iron bar, sticking out from the wall.

Carlos run up the stairs following close behind Pike and away from the deafening screams of the vampires as they slowly burn and drown in the rising holy water.

Sergeant Pike followed by Carlos run from the crypt both dripping wet. Peter looks very concerned but pleased to see them in one piece.

"Are you OK?"

They both nod just catching their breath and taking a moment letting everything sink in. Carlos looks up at Peter with tears in his eyes.

"Tanya, she spoke to me."

Lewis runs over and hugs his dad. He can see his dad is getting upset as tears roll down his cheek. He kisses Lewis on the head.

Pike is sat on the floor and Constable Connor kneels down next to him.

"I'm proud of you."

Pike looks up and smiles.

"Thanks, all in the line of duty."

Constable Connor pats him on the back.

"No, you did really well seriously. Thank you. You have both saved this town and god knows it could have spread if it wasn't for you two."

Pike agrees.

"And do you know the worst thing about this, Constable?"

"What's that, Pike?"

"We can't tell a fucking soul what went on because no one would believe us."

Carlos still upset but pulls himself together for the sake of Lewis. He always has hated being upset in front of him.

Looking at Peter and then turning towards the crypt.

"Tanya spoke to me."

Peter and Lewis listen.

"I had to kill her."

Peter stops him before he walks of.

"No, Carlos, you didn't remember she was already dead."

Lewis looks up at Carlos he also has tears in his eyes. He hates seeing his dad cry and so upset.

"It is true, Dad. We buried Mum, remember?"

Carlos kisses Lewis again on the head.

"Yes, son you're right."

***

The sound of water and agonising screams filled the crypt as the bodies floated on top of the surface.

The water was still bubbling around the vampire's bodies as the holy water destroyed their flesh.

Tanya's corpse was half eaten away by the water. She was only being held up by a thread on the iron spike that she fell on.

Her head slumped to the side revealing her face now mutated by the holy water.

Just her damp hair and sharp fangs and one eye half hanging from the socket was the only thing left of her once pretty face.

Her body eventually collapses and drops into the water causing the water to bubble even more like a boiling kettle. Her body floats and burns as her flesh dissolves.

Chapter Thirty-Eight

The clock in the kitchen is 6:30 pm exactly and Lewis is sitting at the table with Carlos having a snack. Lewis has one of his favourite's beans on toast and Carlos has a ham sandwich and a bag of crisps.

Carlos is sipping on a bottle of beer and Lewis a glass of orange juice.

"Well this time yesterday, we were about to kill a few vampires."

Lewis laughs, "Yeah."

"Can I say something, Dad?"

"Sure."

"And you won't be angry?"

Carlos raises his eyebrows and tilts his head.

"Now, that all depends on what it is?"

Lewis takes a big sigh.

"Oh well, here goes."

Carlos can tell Lewis is going to come out with something handy. Lewis raises his voice imitating his dad.

"And flush the bastards out."

They both fall about laughing. Carlos spits his beer which makes Lewis laugh even more.

"OK, I'll give you that one."

Carlos stands up and grabs a tea towel and wipes the beer from his face and t-shirt.

"I think we both should get an early night and catch up on some sleep. Let's face it, we haven't had much this week."

Lewis finishes his beans on toast while Carlos leans back and watches him eat, sipping occasionally on his bottle of beer.

"Do you know son, I'm really proud of you."

Lewis looks surprised to hear his dad talking like this.

"You are turning into a man. You handled stuff that no man or boy should ever do or see and you stayed strong, stronger than me sometimes I have to admit. I'm proud, son! Really proud!"

Lewis gets up and hugs Carlos. He has tears in his eyes.

"Thanks Dad, I'm proud of you too. I love you."

After a good dose of father and son bonding, Lewis sits back down on his chair and puts his knife and fork together in the centre of the plate just like his mum taught him.

"Can I take my orange juice to bed?"

"Sure, you can."

Lewis puts his plate in the sinks and goes up to bed.

***

Larry locks his tools away in the shed and fastens the padlock and gives it a little shake and pulls just to make sure it's locked tight.

Once again, the moon is full and Larry has worked over hours, almost 11:00 pm and time to lock up again and get on home for some rest.

In the distance, Larry notices the lights go out in the vicarage, a sure sign Peter has gone to bed.

He carries on walking through the churchyard but stops by one of the three empty graves as he notices an old sheet of newspaper. He picks it up and turns, so the moonlight lights up the page just enough for him to read it.

Suddenly Rusty's grave burst open. Larry jumps and shrieks out.

He turns to look down inside the tiny hole, when Rusty jumps out and sinks his fangs into Larry's neck.

Larry rolls around on the ground trying to pull Rusty off, screaming until there was no life left in him.

Rusty runs off into the darkness, leaving Larry's lifeless body in a pool of blood.

THE END